"This is the

"If I can't make ___ ___
tomorrow morning, then my father will go
your talk show. And I'll give him the thumbs up
to embarrass the hell out me. Believe me, not
only will he do so and do it well, he'll enjoy every
second. But if I succeed, then you give me my
interview and we clear the air between us in the
same public way this war started."

"That's big Texas talk and big Texas demands, if I
ever heard them," Darla responded.

His hand traveled a path up her back, to her
neck, under her hair. "Sweetheart, talking isn't
what I have on my mind." His mouth lingered a
breath from hers, tickling her lips and so much
more with promise. "Do we have a deal?"

If it was going to get him to kiss her, and sooner
rather than later, oh yeah, they had a deal.
"Sure," she said. "We have a dea—" His mouth
closed down on hers before she ever got the
final word out.

This was going to be wild.

Blaze

Dear Reader,

I'm so excited to introduce Book 2 of my Stepping Up trilogy. I must admit I've become a real reality-show addict—it ranks right up there with chocolate! I hope you discover some of the magic of these shows in my books.

In *Follow My Lead,* you will meet a new judge on the reality dance show who is at odds with the show's host. The competition between the two results in a few sexy dares, and the fine line between enemies and lovers is soon crossed. I'll be interested to know if you think the dares are as much fun as I did when writing them.

Don't miss the trilogy's exciting conclusion coming next month in *Winning Moves.*

Enjoy!

Lisa Renee Jones

Lisa Renee Jones

FOLLOW MY LEAD

HARLEQUIN®
entertain, enrich, inspire™

Recycling programs
for this product may
not exist in your area.

ISBN-13: 978-0-373-79720-2

FOLLOW MY LEAD

Copyright © 2012 by Lisa Renee Jones

This edition published by arrangement with Harlequin Books S.A.

For questions and comments about the quality of this book please contact us at CustomerService@Harlequin.com.

® and TM are trademarks of Harlequin Enterprises Limited or its corporate affiliates. Trademarks indicated with ® are registered in the United States Patent and Trademark Office, the Canadian Trade Marks Office and in other countries.

www.Harlequin.com

Printed in U.S.A.

ABOUT THE AUTHOR

Lisa spends her days writing the dreams playing in her head. Before becoming a writer, Lisa lived the life of a corporate executive, often taking the red-eye flight out of town and flying home for the excitement of a Little League baseball game. Visit Lisa at www.lisareneejones.com.

Books by Lisa Renee Jones

HARLEQUIN BLAZE
339—HARD AND FAST
442—LONE STAR SURRENDER
559—HOT TARGET
590—JUMP START*
601—HIGH OCTANE*
614—BREATHLESS DESCENT*
710—WATCH ME**

HARLEQUIN NOCTURNE
THE BEAST WITHIN
BEAST OF DESIRE
BEAST OF DARKNESS

  *Texas Hotzone
**Stepping Up

To get the inside scoop on Harlequin Blaze and its talented writers, be sure to check out blazeauthors.com.

All backlist available in ebook. Don't miss any of our special offers. Write to us at the following address for information on our newest releases.

Harlequin Reader Service
U.S.: 3010 Walden Ave., P.O. Box 1325, Buffalo, NY 14269
Canadian: P.O. Box 609, Fort Erie, Ont. L2A 5X3

To my readers, who give me a reason
to get up every day with a smile on my face.
And to my Underground Angels who
spread the love for my books with tender care.

1

DARLA JAMES STOOD IN THE WINDING security line at JFK airport trying not to think about the moment the plane would take off with her inside it. That moment when the massive steel cage, otherwise known as "the plane," would lift into the air with nothing she perceived as logical to keep it from falling to the ground. She pressed her hand to her throat, mentally reprimanding herself. She had to get past this fear of flying if she was going to travel to the various audition cities. Darla had been hired as the new judge on season two of the smash hit *Stepping Up*. The studio was even allowing her to film her morning show on the road, despite it being on a competing network. She wasn't about to blow this opportunity over some dumb fear of flying. She *would* pass through the security gates. She *would not* turn away and run back to her car. This was too big an opportunity for her to mess up, even more so for her parents' struggling ranch and animal shelter.

Darla blew a wayward strand of long blond hair from

her face and noted the televisions hanging from the ceiling. A perky cooking channel goddess was muted, but it was clear that she was describing how to make a strawberry cake. Darla welcomed the distraction the show offered, telling herself that she might recreate that perfect masterpiece in her own kitchen. Although she was better known for burning a grilled cheese sandwich or two.

By the time Darla made it past the metal detectors, she was eager to double-check her stock of necessities for the flight. She should have a package of Hershey's kisses, her favorite romance author's latest book and her headphones. Anything not easily spotted per a quick inspection would be purchased at the gift shop. Those items represented her best hope that she wouldn't embarrass herself on the plane. Anything to avoid wayward yelps during takeoff or panicked questions about the sounds the plane might make. She'd been there, done that, and received the dirty looks of those who were not afraid to fly. She hated those looks.

The plastic bin containing her things slid to a halt in front of her and with her in place and fifteen minutes to spare before boarding, Darla whirled toward departures. That was when she was hit with her first wave of turbulence. Coming face-to-face with Blake Nelson—her show nemesis—or rather, face-to-chest with him, considering the man was a good foot taller than her measly five foot two inches, was bad news. She swallowed hard, not having to look beyond the navy T-shirt stretching across an impressive chest to be convinced of Blake's good looks. She already got his appeal thanks to another up-close-and-personal occasion she wished she could forget.

Darla tore her gaze from his impressive set of pecs. She wondered what her weakness for a man who had been downright mean to her a few months before said about her. Sadly, she concluded that her producer, Kayla—two years her senior at twenty-nine and happily married to a gorgeous veterinarian—was right. Darla must really have a secret, self-defeating mechanism when it came to relationships. She was attracted to all the wrong men.

Blake's brilliant blue gaze captured hers and twinkled in a moment of mischief before he glanced down at her socked feet peeking beneath her blue jeans. He arched a dark brow. "I always seem to catch you with your shoes off."

She grimaced at the reference to their "incident" as she thought of it, in which they'd been working a red carpet event, side by side, when her heel had broken off her shoe. She'd proceeded to stumble happily against that hard body of his. He'd reciprocated by catching her and flirting outrageously. Unfortunately, his camera crew had captured the entire embarrassing event on film.

"I'd have thought you'd gotten the shoe jokes out of your system when you made fun of me on your show the next morning," she muttered, and then marched toward the line of chairs just past security and sat down.

He followed, stopping in front of her—or rather, towering over her. She refused to look up at him and instead, infuriatingly, noticed his powerful thighs flex beneath his jeans. Not that his muscles—or that sexy cleft in his chin mattered. He was not the man for her.

"My guest made fun of you," he said, as if that gave him some form of defense. "Not me."

Her gaze jerked to his, anger brought her back to her senses. "You played the footage of our exchange on *your* show. *Your* guest—Rick—was the host of *Stepping Up* not *The Blake Nelson Show*. He didn't have the power to make that happen."

"Rick plotted with my producer who was fishing for ratings. I told him off and my producer. And I called you to apologize."

She laced one of her boots, seeing no reason to deny that he'd called. "I didn't want to talk to you any more than I want to work with Rick. But we don't always get what we want."

Surprise registered on his chiseled, too-handsome, arrogant face. "Are you always so honest?"

She stood up. "With appropriate discretion—which means not at the risk of hurting someone. What you and Rick did to me could have hurt my career and my livelihood. You made me look like I wasn't focused on my job, like I was playing games on the red carpet. And, no, it didn't get me fired, but had my ratings dipped, it would have been brought up again, and you know it." It certainly had made her doubt her desire to be in the public eye. She threw the strap of her bag over her shoulder. "And for the record, I didn't take your call because I was afraid our conversation would later become

a part of your show. I have to run to catch my flight."
She started walking.

He fell into step beside her a bit too easily, as if he'd
anticipated the move. She glared up at him, quickly turning away before those blue eyes captured hers, sending
a flutter to her stomach. "Why are you following me?"

He ignored the question. "If it's any consolation, not
only did that show's content not hurt your career, your
fans—and mine, for that matter—were furious with me.
I got hate mail and the phones rang off the hook for
weeks after. My viewers thought the incident was just
as inappropriate as you did."

She knew that because she'd gotten her share of mail,
as well. And that mail had been what had kept her from
quitting. That—and her family who, as always, loved
and supported her. "What you did was inappropriate."
She cut him a look. "But I assume your ratings softened the blow of the outcry." They'd been huge—off
the charts.

He threw up his hands. "I didn't have anything to do
with what happened. I swear to you, Darla. I would never
have done something so callous. If you replay the footage
of my show you'll see the shock on my face. And you'll
see I tried to salvage the situation while I was on air."

Dang. He sounded sincere. So sincere that… *Don't
do it,* she silently warned herself. Don't fall victim to the
wrong guy saying the right things. She wanted to do it,
too, she wanted to believe him, to stop and tell him that
it was okay, that it was old history, because that is what

she did. She made people feel better, she forgave them. She lay down and let them walk all over her.

Knowing how close she was to making a huge mistake with this man, Darla all but shouted with joy at the sight of a ladies' room. She had her escape from Mr. Wrong.

Darla stopped abruptly. "Excuse me, but I have to run in here."

"Wait, Darla. There's something—"

"Sorry," she said, knowing if he talked one minute more or kept looking at her with those damnable gorgeous eyes, she'd start caving in again. She motioned behind her. "No men allowed." Cringing at the silly statement—like he didn't know no men were allowed?—she rushed down the narrow, tiled hallway.

The instant Darla was out of Blake's sight, she slumped against the wall, unaware that she'd been holding her breath. He was just one heck of a lot of man. And there was no question that it would be easy for her to forget why she had to be on guard around him, forget he was her enemy.

She pushed off the wall and plopped her bag down on the corner of a long counter running beneath a mirror. She'd vowed to lay off the Easter chocolate, which always meant an extra five pounds, and the wrong men, which usually amounted to an extra seven. The camera was pretty darn unforgiving, which helped strengthen her otherwise weak promise. There was no Blake Nelson anywhere in her future but as a competitor for ratings.

There was, however, something to look forward to.

Though her show wasn't a money-maker, not yet, she still sent every dime she could home. *Stepping Up* could solve all her problems by giving her enough to pay off her parents' debt and get them ahead. *If* Darla made it through the first four episodes. That's when the reality show's executives either had to call her a one-season wonder or take up the option, guaranteeing her one more season with a big fat bonus. Even if they didn't option her, she hoped she'd have enough of a ratings boost on her morning show to increase her pay there.

Darla shoved Blake and worries over the future out of her mind and focused on the urgent matter at hand. She did an inventory of her bag for the flight to Denver, the first audition city. Chocolate—check. Book—check. *Oh, no.* Where were her headphones? She had to have her headphones so she wouldn't hear the sounds the plane made. A frantic search proved they weren't there and she cringed when she remembered reminding herself to grab them off the kitchen table.

She snatched up her bag and headed for the exit, intending to search out the gift shop, not even thinking about Blake. That was until she was out the door and felt a rush of disappointment that he was gone. Clearly, she was so not over her Mr. Wrong guy syndrome. Nor, she realized five minutes later, was she going to have a headset for the flight. Darla charged down the walkway, and just that one chink in her travel armor had her fear soaring. What if they crashed? What if the engine stopped working? What about birds?

She halted at the gangway to the plane and handed

the stewardess her boarding pass. The woman scanned it and smiled. "Welcome, Ms. James. You'll be in a window seat on the fourth row and I'll be by to check on you momentarily."

"Thank you," she said, and wondered if the reality show had put her in first class because it was safer. That had to be it. Why else would they spend such a ridiculous amount of money on a seat not so unlike the others a few rows behind? She inhaled, and fought the urge to ask the stewardess the millions of questions rushing through her mind—like how experienced the pilot was and how much rest he'd had.

Forcefully, she sent a command to her legs to move, to walk through the entry and down the aisle. And that's when the second wave of turbulence hit her, because Blake Nelson was sitting in the seat next to hers.

2

"I TRIED TO WARN YOU," Blake said, doing his best not to smile at the adorably distressed expression on Darla James's face. He could see why the Colorado country girl gone big city had charmed her audience into a top ratings slot. He was as taken with her as her viewers were, something no woman had done to him in a very long time, he realized.

"Warn me?" she asked, blinking in confusion and shoving a lock of blond hair from her eyes to see him more clearly.

"Right," he said, unable to keep himself from teasing her. "When you tucked tail and ran into the bathroom." And it became abundantly clear that she didn't know he was taking the trip with her.

"I did not tuck…" Understanding slid across her lovely heart-shaped face. "You were going to warn me that we were traveling together?" He gave a slow nod and her pale green eyes glinted with yellow flecks, then narrowed on him suspiciously as she, no doubt, began to put two and two together. "How would you have known we were on the same flight, next to each other, unless…"

The same person made our reservations, he finished silently for her. Noting the flight attendant approaching her from behind, he suggested, "I think you need to sit down." He stood up to let her by and reached for her bag. "Do you want me to put that overhead?"

"I'll keep it and I don't need to sit. I need you to tell me what is going on."

"Hello, Ms. James," the flight attendant said, drawing her attention. "Is there a problem? I need to clear the aisle for boarding. I can help you with your bag if you need help?"

"I… No. No problem." She turned a perplexed look on Blake, her ivory cheeks now flushed a pretty pink. "I guess I need to sit down."

His lips twitched and he motioned her forward. "Probably a good idea."

She scooted into the seat by the window and Blake quickly took his seat, the soft scent of her floral perfume hung in the air—sweet like the woman. He was really ready for sweet, and someone with her own career, her own dreams, instead of the women who chased his success or his money.

She whirled on him, her tartness doing nothing to sour her sweetness. "What's going on?"

"I work for the same network as *Stepping Up,*" he said, stating the obvious. "I'm filming a special segment on the first audition stop."

She inhaled and exhaled, her fingers curling around

her bag, which she clutched in her lap. "I'd have thought someone would have warned me."

"Well," he said. "I did the same thing last year. They probably assumed you knew that since we have competing morning shows. I guess I should warn you that I'll be back the first week the finalists move into the contestant house to film the reality portion of the show. Then again when the winner is announced and gets the studio contract and the two hundred and fifty thousand dollar prize. And, for the record, I doubt the studio thought you'd react quite so…shall we say *intensely* to my presence, since you're the one with the new cable contract."

"I was surprised, not *intense*," she countered. "Whatever intense is supposed to mean."

He glanced down at her bag. "You're holding on to that bag like you either plan to hit me with it or make a run for the door."

"Hitting you with my bag would bring me a lot of joy after what you did to me a few months ago," she said. "Unfortunately, it would also bring unwanted attention and trouble, so I'll settle for simply fantasizing about it. It'll distract me from the run to the door. And I'll just tell you right now that I don't like to fly. You might want to consider changing seats with someone. I'm going to drive you bonkers. Then again, maybe you should stay. This trip will be my revenge for your past sins."

"Ah," he said. "You're a control freak."

"I'm not a control freak."

"People who don't like to fly are control freaks."

"I'm *not* a control freak. And by the way, before I

forget and you think I didn't catch what you said—you wouldn't have felt the need to 'warn me' if you didn't think I was going to react intensely to you being here."

"I thought you said you didn't react intensely?"

"Your word, not mine."

"Can I get you two something to drink?" the flight attendant asked, stopping beside them.

"A glass of champagne," Darla said quickly.

Blake frowned. "It's ten in the morning."

"Then make it a mimosa," she told the attendant, then to Blake, "That has orange juice in it. I wasn't joking when I said I was a bad flyer and, honestly, I'm not a good drinker, either, but it's better than a sedative." She glanced back at the attendant. "In fact, you better bring him one, too. Actually, you might want to have one yourself because you were unlucky enough to have me on this flight."

Blake laughed along with the attendant and nodded his approval. "Bring me one, thanks."

The attendant glanced at Darla's bag. "It needs to go under your seat for takeoff."

Darla unzipped it and handed Blake a bag of chocolate. "Hold this, please." Next she handed him a book. "And this."

He glanced at the romance novel and read the title. "*Dangerous Passion* by Lisa Renee Jones?"

She shoved her bag under her seat and buckled her seat belt. "Paranormal with a hot military hero who is going to save the world and his woman." She grabbed the candy and the book. "It's for the book club on my show. You got a problem with romance?"

"Not at all," he chuckled. "In fact, maybe I need to send a few to my sister. She falls for losers and then wonders why they walk all over her. I'd rather she find a hero in a book than try and turn someone into one that isn't."

"Your sister and I should talk," she murmured. He would have asked about that loaded comment, but she quickly added, "And on that note, not one word we exchange on this flight better end up on your show. If you turn my fear into a joke, I swear to you—"

"I won't," he said, capturing her gaze, trying to let her see the truth in his. "I wouldn't do something like that."

"Mimosas have arrived," the attendant said. "But drink up quickly. We'll be getting underway soon."

Blake accepted the drinks and handed one to Darla. She reached for the glass, their fingers touched, and damn if he didn't know that touch. She felt it, too, that connection they'd had on the red carpet. A connection that he'd fully intended to act upon, if not for the disaster on his show the following morning. He'd been hot for this woman then, and time hadn't changed that. Hot and hard, and remarkably getting harder from nothing more than the idea of touching her, holding her as he had when she'd fallen against him. He was going to hold her again, all right, and this time without an audience. There was something about this woman that made him want to know her and that was something he hadn't felt in a very long time.

He lifted his glass. "To new beginnings."

She studied him a moment and clinked her glass to his. "To new beginnings." And suddenly, the plane's engines started.

"Oh, God," Darla exclaimed. All the heat and fire in her stare turned into panic.

"I promise you," he said, strongly contemplating the likelihood that kissing her right now as a means of distraction would end with him getting punched. "Everything's fine. If it makes you feel any better, my father's a retired commercial pilot, so I've flown a lot." He glanced down at her drink, but not before he noticed, and not for the first time, the small, sexy mole just above her lip. Damn, he liked that mole. "This might be a good time to drink that mimosa."

She downed it. "Can I have another?"

He handed her his. "I thought you said you weren't a good drinker?"

She downed his drink. "I'm not. I need to eat something." She tore open the chocolate.

"Chocolate isn't food."

"Chocolate absolutely is food." She laughed. "Oh, boy. I'm already feeling a buzz." She sank in her seat and cut him a look. "Did I mention that you should probably find another seat?" The stewardess came by and took the empty glasses while another began the standard instructional chatter.

"You did," he assured her. "And I refused." The plane started to move and she sat bolt upright to look out of the window.

"Oh, no," he said, easing her back. "Don't watch. That's the worst thing you can do."

"I have to watch," she said, glowering at him. "And how would you know that's the worst thing I can do?"

"Because my mother was afraid of flying," he said, trying to distract her. "And she is one hundred percent a control freak. I bet you balance your checkbook every day." He shoved down the window shade.

"Doesn't everyone?"

"I don't."

"Well, that's a mistake." She glowered. "Let go of the window shade."

"If you don't look out of the window you won't know whether or not to question if it's normal or not."

"I told you. I have to look."

"That's what my mother said, too, and then she tried it with the shade down and it worked. She relaxed instead of spending the entire flight in a tense ball of nerves. Now she's a travel writer."

"I'm not your mother."

"No," he said softly, his hand dropping from the window, and settling on her leg. "You are most definitely *not* my mother. And believe me, I am very aware of that fact." Sexual tension crackled between them, as good a distraction as he could ever hope for. Then the damnable wheels growled beneath the plane, retracting.

"Oh, my God," she whispered, "did we just take off?"

He flipped up the armrest between them. "Yes," he answered, turning so that he faced her fully. "See how fast things happen when you aren't watching every little movement? How about opening that chocolate?"

"I need to look—"

He ran his hand down her arm, keeping her toward him. "Look at me."

Her eyes met his and the connection was instant. He didn't remember the last time a woman made his blood boil with nothing more than a look. But this one sure did. "You need another strategy to deal with your fear, other than mimosas and chocolate, if you're going to make the twenty-city audition schedule."

"Thirty," she corrected.

"Thirty," he repeated. "That's a lot of cities. It's going to be hard to keep up that pace if you stay this uptight. Try it my way. Stay away from the window and focus on other things. *Like me.*"

"I think focusing on you is a bad idea."

"And why is that?"

"Because I've been drinking and I might forget how much I don't like you."

"Or alternatively," he suggested, "you might remember that you actually *do* like me."

THAT'S EXACTLY WHAT SHE WAS worried about. Liking him. Forgetting why she shouldn't. Forgetting he was just another one of the power-hungry, driven men who attracted her, but later left her emotions bruised. He'd proven that by using her for better ratings. Blake was far more the wrong guy than any of the wrong guys before him, because he could impact her career. She'd been clipped by his potential power already and survived. Next time she might not. So, knowing all of this, why, why, *why* was she staring at his mouth, wishing he'd kiss her and distract her from the window? Didn't she care that they were in a semipublic place?

"You might even decide that you want to kiss me," he said, as if reading her mind. He leaned in closer, so that the spicy male scent of him teased her nostrils.

There was no "might" about wanting to kiss him. It was all she could do not to press her lips to his, which was a clear indication that a mimosa was not the way to cope with travel—or Blake Nelson.

"I'm not going to look at you or out the window." She shifted in her seat and put her tray table down, setting the bag of chocolate on top and grabbing her book. "I'll read." She opened up her romance novel and began reading from where she'd left off.

She shoved him to his back, straddled him. Kissed him. Wild didn't begin to describe what kissing Lara unleashed inside Damion. One minute they were kissing, the next they were touching, licking, tasting. Her naked backside rubbing against his cock drove him insane with need. He couldn't get enough of her. Couldn't make himself stop kissing her, caressing her, couldn't resist molding her breasts in his hands and swallowing the moan that slid from her lips to his. They melted into one another, the play of tongue against tongue, and wildness turned into an unfamiliar desperation

like nothing he had ever experienced with another
woman, a need to escape into each other, a need
not to speak, not to think.

Damion's hand slid up her back, into her hair,
angling her mouth to deepen the kiss, to take more.
Whatever happened beyond this moment, beyond
the desire, didn't matter. There was no right or
wrong, no enemies or even friends—there was just
feeling, needing, taking.

Darla set the book down. *No enemies or even friends.*
That passage was just a little too close to what she
wanted to happen with Blake. This was so not the answer
to resisting Blake Nelson. She reached for the bag of
chocolate and unwrapped a piece, not looking at Blake,
but she could feel him looking at her. She was about to
stick the first Hershey's kiss into her mouth when the
plane jolted. She yelped and the candy—the piece in her
hand, and the entire bag—went flying.

Blake captured the bag and pushed her tray up, turning her toward him again. "Turbulence is nothing to
worry about. Once you've been on a few really bad
flights you realize just how much a plane can take."

The attendant rushed over to them. "Everything
okay?"

"Is it?" Darla asked.

"Of course, honey," she said. "Bumps are normal.
It's August. This time of year, hot air pockets create
turbulence."

"You're sure?" Darla asked, watching her expression

closely for signs she, indeed, was not sure but didn't want to say as much.

"I'm positive."

"Two more mimosas when you can, please," Blake said, his focus on Darla. "If you get drunk, I promise to get you to your room, and I won't take advantage of you, no matter how much I want to."

3

HE WOULDN'T TAKE ADVANTAGE of her, no matter how much he wanted to. That was the statement Blake had made that had opened the door of possibility for Darla, the one that spoke of honor, of a good man. Maybe she really had misjudged him. Maybe she was so conditioned to believe she always chose the wrong men that she was looking for flaws in Blake unfairly.

"Here you go," the flight attendant said. "Two more mimosas."

Blake passed Darla her drink and kept one for himself.

"Actually," Darla said. "I think we need to even the stakes here. I've had two. These two are yours."

He arched a brow and then eased his shoulder back into the seat, still facing her, his voice low and intimate. "I really will take care of you if you want to drink that."

"I believe you. How old is your sister? Younger or older?"

"Younger by five years," he said. "She's twenty-seven."

"And here I thought the wrong man syndrome was a curse for show business types. Maybe it's the curse of the twenty-seven-year-olds."

"I love the hell out of my sister, but she has issues way beyond age. Namely, she needs to act hers—but that's a long story that would require a few extra mimosas. And you and I, well, we aren't exactly in an industry that's relationship friendly. It's populated with a lot of people who are out for number one. That has to be different from the life you were living as the Colorado rancher's daughter."

"I still live life as a Colorado rancher's daughter," she said. "And the minute this business makes me something else, I'm out."

"You might not know when it happens," he suggested. "Most people don't."

"My family will know and they'll knock some sense into me."

He smiled. "Same with mine."

"You're close to your family?"

"Very. It was my father's investment strategies that got me here to begin with. I started doing YouTube investment segments about the stock market while I was in college, which began with too much tequila and a dare." He lifted his glass and took a sip. "Luckily I handle my alcohol better at thirty-two than I did at twenty-one. The first video was such a hit that I kept doing them, and somehow, someone who mattered saw them and the rest is history. That's how I ended up writing that handbook for investing in the stock market and why it's a regular feature on my show."

"You highlight stocks on your show and I highlight romance novels," she observed. "Like night and day."

"Which is why there's an audience for both of us," he said. "Sometimes people want business advice and sometimes they just need to escape. Sometimes the same person might want one thing one day and the other the next."

She'd thought the same thing many times. "You'll never convince my network of that. They want me to take you down."

His eyes—so brilliantly blue—twinkled with mischief. "And what about you? Do you want to take me down?"

"After you made a fool of me on your show, I did," she admitted.

"I didn't—"

"I'm willing to accept that maybe—just maybe—you weren't responsible for what happened," she conceded.

"Maybe?"

"That's all you're getting from me right now."

"It's better than the outright hatred I got from you earlier, so I'll take the maybe." He downed the drink. "You know, this is a three-hour flight. You can drink another mimosa and still not have to worry about what happens when we get off the plane."

She was more worried about what wouldn't happen if she drank. Meaning, she wanted him to know that if their flirtation went beyond this flight, she was clear-headed. Not that she was planning to do anything with this man. Still…options were good.

She took his empty glass from him and handed him her full one. "I'll consider another drink when you're one up on me."

He hit the attendant button. "Then I better get busy." He downed her drink.

She laughed. "I thought you weren't going to get me drunk and take advantage of me?"

"That's exactly why I need to get you drunk," he assured her. "So you'll be safe. But just in case you're wondering, I'm okay with you getting *me* drunk and taking advantage of me."

She laughed again but right at that moment, the plane jolted back and forth. Her heart lurched and she grabbed his leg. "Easy," he murmured, his hand closing over hers. "Just the heat—remember?" He eased closer so that their knees were touching. "You're perfectly safe right now."

Heat. Oh, yes. There was heat—plenty of heat screaming a path through her body, making every nerve ending she had tingle with awareness.

"Hi," the flight attendant said.

Blake glanced at Darla. "Another drink?"

"Only if I eat first."

"We're actually about to serve brunch," the attendant said, and proceeded to give them their meal choices.

Once they'd ordered, Blake turned back to Darla, still holding her hand. She stared down at his. He had big, strong hands. Hands that made her think of him touching her.

"Now where were we?" he asked, drawing her gaze. "Oh, yes. Talking about you getting me drunk and taking advantage of me. But since I'm barely above getting beaten with your bag, I'm pretty sure that's not going to happen. So why don't you tell me how your show got started?"

The plane shook and she inhaled, quickly diving into her reply to keep herself from diving for the window shade instead. "I was at the University of Colorado with my sights set on a journalism degree. I took a drama class thinking it would be a fun, easy elective that would allow me time for the college paper. The next thing I knew I was writing scripts and producing a school play. Long story short, I ended up working for a casting director in New York and met with a producer looking for a new morning-show host."

"And the producer decided it should be you."

"Yes, but I said no at first. I was terrified to be in front of the camera. I still am half the time. I have silly things happen, like when I spilled water all over Miss Universe, who'd come on the show to support a children's charity." She cringed. "I suppose if they didn't fire me over that I shouldn't have thought they'd fire me over my broken shoe. I just keep worrying they'll realize I'm not meant to be on camera."

"Those things make your audience love you, you know," he said softly. "It's part of that country-girl-gone-big-city charm."

She felt her cheeks flush red. "Thank you. But seriously, my show is less than a year old. It's hard to feel like I belong here. It's all just so...surreal."

"Well, you do, and clearly the powers that be for *Stepping Up* see that, too."

"Yeah, well, did I mention that I was the assistant casting director who found Rick the job as host for *Stepping Up?* And yes, I mean Rick—as in the guest who used my broken shoe as fodder on your show."

His eyes went wide. "You're freaking kidding me."

"Nope," she said. "I got him the job, and still he used me. That's what really got to me about the whole thing, I think."

"Funny," he said. "I kind of thought it had something to do with you maybe thinking that we had a connection that you then questioned. I know I thought we had a connection."

She inhaled, taken off guard. She had. God, had she ever. She liked him. Too much. She still did.

"Food's here," the attendant said, sparing her from a reply.

Darla sat up, quick to break eye contact with Blake, not sure what she was feeling right now. Alcohol, an empty stomach and an airplane. She was not in a position to be making decisions about men, especially this one.

It wasn't as if her track record was stellar even on her best day, and this wasn't one of them. She'd dated one player after another since moving to New York, even before her show, until she was so afraid of becoming jaded, she'd simply stopped dating. There was just something about Blake, something that made her want to try again, and that scared her because it had hurt when she'd thought he'd used her for ratings. Hurt more than it should have, which told her that he could possibly break her heart. Which was why she had to get control of the situation, and of herself.

So as soon as she and Blake had plates in front of them, she quickly picked up the conversation in comfortable territory. "Back to *Stepping Up,*" she said. "I not only helped them find Rick, I also did some pre-screening of the dancers for the first season, including three that made the top ten. That's how this came about, how I got the job offer to be a judge."

"And now you're going to be working with Rick."

"Yeah," she said. "Now I get to work with that jerk."

He laughed. "I agree. He's a jerk. And I told him so after my show."

"So did I," she admitted with a smile.

"So you took his call but not mine?"

"He didn't call," she said, stabbing an egg with her fork. "I called him."

"But you wouldn't talk to me?"

"No," she said. "I wouldn't talk to you."

"I would have gladly let you call me a jerk to have the chance to explain what had happened."

And she would have let him explain, and would have forgiven him. Like she was now. The conversation continued, and more and more she laughed and relaxed. When finally their plates were gone, she had changed her tune about Blake, about where this was—or was not—going. They had one night and then she'd be flying from city to city, absorbed in filming the reality show. It wasn't as if this attraction could become anything more serious. There were really only two ways this flight could end: Darla in her room alone, or Darla in her room with Blake.

Tomorrow would be the same no matter what—they would be hundreds of miles apart. She wanted him. She wanted him like no other that she could ever remember. And she wasn't letting anything—including too many mimosas—get in her way. He might be a mirage, the wrong man once again hidden beneath hot, sexy perfection. But tonight, she decided right then and there, she was going to make him hers.

4

NEAR SEVEN IN THE EVENING, Blake and Darla stood in front of the arrivals terminal, waiting for their car, battling the chilly gusting Denver wind.

Blake inhaled the delicate floral scent of Darla's perfume, the feminine sweetness like whiskey warming his limbs. He rarely noticed a woman's perfume. But then, Darla wasn't just any other woman. He wasn't sure of the exact moment, sometime after she'd traded in her mimosas for coffee and before the bumpy landing, when she'd desperately clung to her seat and then momentarily to him, he'd realized she had, and still was, effortlessly seducing him.

"I can't believe I forgot it would be this cold already," Darla said, fighting an obvious shiver. "And I darn sure can't believe there isn't a cab to be found. This is an international airport. It's just strange."

"Mountain country gets cold at night by most standards, even during the summer. Will you be seeing your parents on this trip?"

"I wish," she added. "But they're tied up with the ranch and hours away. We're here and gone so fast I won't have the time." She motioned to a line of cabs rounding the corner.

"Looks like someone opened the flood gates," he commented.

A four-door black sedan pulled up at the curb in front of them and the driver quickly exited and spoke over the roof. "So sorry, Ms. James and Mr. Nelson. There's a traffic accident on the highway leading into the airport." He popped the trunk. "I'll put your bags in the back."

Blake reached for Darla's large suitcase—large as in the size of Texas. "You better let me get that for you." He rolled it to the rear of the vehicle and hefted it into the compartment. "Good gosh, woman. This thing weighs a ton. You might want to rethink such a huge bag for so much travel. Next time I won't be here."

She scoffed. "Only a man would suggest such a thing. I'm going to thirty cities and a girl needs good shoes to be on television." She grimaced. "There's a way to bring up bad memories."

Somehow, he was going to live down the past. "One of many reasons I'm glad I'm a man. Shoe choices are simple." He opened the back door for her and waved her in. "Ladies first."

She slid inside and Blake joined her. Again in close quarters with Darla, his blood thrummed with anticipation. Darla definitely gave him another reason to be happy he was a man right now.

"Might as well get comfortable, folks," the driver suggested. "We're a good forty-five minutes from downtown."

"Yikes," Darla said, glancing at her watch. "I was supposed to meet my producer for drinks at 8:30 p.m."

"Meagan Kellar?" Blake asked, confirming they were both talking about the show's creator, and whose husband was the studio's head of security.

"Yes," she said. "You, too?"

He nodded. "I doubt it will matter if we're late. It's probably a large group."

"Still," Darla said, clearly concerned, "maybe I should call her."

"Sorry to interrupt," the driver said. "But I did send a text message to Ms. Kellar when I arrived at the airport, per her request."

"Oh, excellent," Darla said. "Thank you so much."

Blake found her quick, polite response sincere and refreshing. She was like a cool drink of water in the midst of what had become the murky water of people with agendas, whether they be work-related or personal. He wasn't sure most people separated the two. Darla was who Darla was, untouched by success, free of airs and a big ego, and thankfully without fake niceties.

"You know," he said, "I'm glad you got mad at me when you first saw me in the airport."

She gave him an inquisitive look. "You're glad I got mad at you?"

"That's right," he said. "Nothing like someone who hates you smiling to your face and cursing you behind your back."

"Well, I don't hate you," she said, and then smiled, "Not since my second mimosa."

"And did that feeling remain intact after coffee number two?"

"Shockingly," she teased, "it did."

Darla's cell phone started to ring. "If we were at one of the Denver casinos, I'd bet you this is my mother calling." She glanced at the number and held up the screen. "My mother. She knows I hate to fly but then so does everyone after today, right?" Darla shook her head. "I have to get over that." She answered the call and he could hear her mother asking about her trip, how she was doing, what happened next. Darla glanced at Blake, a cute, playful expression on her face. And sexy. Damn, the woman was adorably sexy, which was not a combination he'd often come across. "Would you believe Blake Nelson is here?" she asked, continuing her conversation with her mother.

"What?" Blake heard her mother through the phone. "That jerk that made fun of you on cable television?"

Blake arched a brow and Darla laughed, her eyes dancing with mischief. "I don't know if I'd call him a jerk."

"You did call him a jerk," her mother said. "And with good reason."

"Yeah," she admitted. "I did call him a jerk but I was upset at the time." They talked a bit more and Darla hung up. "She's protective. So is my dad."

"I kind of gathered that." He settled against the door

to face her. "Have you revised your thoughts on me being a jerk?"

"I've decided not to judge the host by his guest," she teased, leaning on her door as well and studying him. "With caution, that is."

"What if I buy you dinner as a peace offering?"

She frowned. "My dinners are paid for by the show."

He laughed. "Okay, so that wasn't my best foot forward. What did you have in mind?"

Her brows furrowed. "My mom says she never wants anything that she doesn't come by honestly, and I live by that. I'm not suggesting anything."

"And my mother would say bring chocolate or don't come at all," he quipped. "But you brought your own."

"What would your father say?"

"Have you seen any of my father's visits on my show?"

She shook her head. "No. I didn't know your father visits your show. That's actually really amazing that you are close enough to him to have him on."

"Yeah, well, the audience loves him. He's an ex-rodeo bull rider who now runs a chain of rodeo-themed bars. My mother used to do promotional work for the rodeo. Now she does damage control for his big mouth. You'd never guess the man has a golden stock portfolio he handles himself, which he talks about on my show in a colorful way. *Which* is part of what makes my viewers love him. But we have to bleep him at least once every time he visits. In other words, if we're looking for advice on peace offerings, my father's suggestions would probably get me in hot water. Maybe we should stick with your mother's wise words."

"Well," she said, laughing, "I think your father sounds wonderful, but my mother does have one other piece of wisdom that seems fairly appropriate." Her eyes dazzled with a combination of mischief, mayhem and enough sizzling heat to set his seat—and him—on fire.

He was intrigued. "What would that be?"

She leaned closer, her red-tinged lush lips curved slightly upward. "You get what you give." He smiled at the suggestive words. She smiled back. "You'll have to use your imagination from there."

His imagination was well into overdrive, not needing a nudge one bit—in fact, it went as wild as he wanted to with her. "I should warn you that my imagination is about as active as my father's colorful words."

"Well then," she said approvingly, "I guess I better have big expectations." His cell phone chose that inopportune moment, when his blood was pumping hot, to ring. He grabbed it from his belt, intending to shut it up so he could get back to working his imagination, but no such luck. It was his producer.

"My producer," he told her, "who isn't happy that the studio brought me here without my crew." He answered the call and listened to a laundry list of notes for the next day's interviews. Then a long list of questions followed, one of which had him glancing at Darla and smiling. "What are my chances of getting an interview with Darla James? I'll get back to you on that."

He would most definitely regret letting what might be

a once-in-a-lifetime opportunity with Darla slip away—
but not the on-camera kind. The up-close-and-personal
and absolutely private kind.

"I'LL GIVE YOU AN INTERVIEW on one condition," Darla
said when Blake ended his call.

"Let me guess," he said, his blue eyes glinting humor
and intelligence. "You want to interview *me* for your
show? The whole 'you get what you give' concept,
right?"

"Now you're getting the idea," Darla said with approval. She still couldn't believe she had flirted so
openly with Blake. But to her surprise, she was incredibly comfortable with her now-past nemesis. "Besides,
I think it would be fun. Our audiences would eat it up."

"Here we are," the driver said, pulling into a hotel
parking lot.

Darla frowned. "I thought we were staying at the
Rocky Mountain Tower?"

"My apologies, ma'am," the driver said, glancing
in the mirror at her. "I thought you knew about the
change of plans. Apparently, the paparazzi are all over
the Tower, looking for the new judges. The studio felt
you'd have more privacy here, at least for the time being,
away from where the auditions are happening and where
the press won't be on your back."

"Oh," she said, not sure what to make of that. "Paparazzi?"

"You seem surprised," Blake said curiously. "The

ratings for *Stepping Up* were huge last season. You're about to walk into the middle of a hurricane."

"Yes, of course," she agreed, trying to sound calm. She didn't feel calm. The magnitude of this endeavor hit her like a ton of bricks. It could change her life, her family's life. She didn't want to blow this. She wasn't going to let them sell everything, or allow the ranch to be taken over by the bank, whichever came first. "That makes sense."

"'That makes sense'?" Blake repeated, nudging her. "Your choice of words says this isn't what you expected. And why do you now look like you want to be sick? What's wrong?"

She jerked her gaze to Blake's, realizing she'd been staring at the back of the driver's seat. "That obvious?"

"You're pretty transparent," Blake said as the driver parked the car.

Darla crinkled her nose. "I really need to work on that."

The driver opened her door. "Home sweet hotel," he said, waving her outside.

She glanced at Blake, trying to shake off her panic over the show, and gravely joked, "See you on the outside." She scooted out of the car and headed for the trunk, where Blake met her. And oh, was the man sexy, a handsome blend of rough-edged good looks and charming grace. If anyone could keep her mind off tomorrow's first day on camera, this man could.

"I'll get your bags to your rooms," the driver offered and handed them both small packets. She noted a number on the front of each. "These are your room keys, which work the elevator, as well. Your room numbers are on the envelopes. You'll both be going to floor eighteen. That's a private floor. And drinks with Ms. Kellar and her party will be in the lounge area of eighteen, as well."

Darla blinked at that. "Thank you. That's wonderful." Blake slid the man a tip and the driver gave them a quick formal bow before departing.

They entered the hotel and went directly to the bank of elevators. Blake punched the elevator button and checked an incoming text, quickly sending back a reply and then another, before putting away his phone. "You're not afraid of heights, are you? Eighteen is a fairly high floor."

She pursed her lips. "Not when there are windows and walls."

He chuckled. "No skydiving for you then?"

"Uh," she said, "No. No skydiving for me."

"Hmm," he murmured, giving her a thoughtful inspection that did nothing to diminish the heat in his gaze. "I think we should make a bet and if I win you go skydiving with me. There's plenty of gorgeous jump locations in Colorado."

"You did see me inside that plane, right?" she asked, giving him an appalled look. "I was the white-knuckled one who dug her fingernails into your hand, I held on so tight." The elevator doors opened.

He smiled. "I do seem to have a vague memory of fingernail-induced pain, but that's just all the more reason to face fear and conquer it. I promise you, once you skydive you'll be over the flying phobia."

She entered the empty car and he followed. "By jumping out of a plane? Are you now going to tell me that's how your mother got over her fear? What happened to the window shade theory?"

"I plead the fifth," he said, slipping his key card into a slot on the wall and punching the button for the eighteenth floor.

"There you go," she said decisively. "You didn't talk her into it and you won't talk me into it. No skydiving."

"You'll have a parachute in place. Besides, you don't even know what the bet is. You might win."

"I never make a bet I'm afraid to lose."

"You do know you get to pick the prize if you win."

The prize. Oh, yeah, she could think of some really interesting prizes. Like a thousand orgasms. She laughed mischievously, unable to stop herself. This was her opening, her way to make him hers for the night, if she could find the courage to be daring.

He shrugged. "Care to let me in on whatever that secret is? It looks worth knowing, based on your reaction."

"I was just thinking of what that prize might be." She'd almost been daring, but not quite. The butterflies in her stomach got the best of her.

"I'm guessing from your pleased little giggle that your prize most likely involves my embarrassment as payback for your shoe."

"I'm over the shoe," she assured him. "And I am not looking to embarrass you." But unbidden, an image of herself falling off her shoe and into Blake flashed in her mind. What if she was letting their short time together make her too trusting, too naive? The butt of a shoe joke was one thing. The butt of a bedroom joke could be truly career ending.

"The longer you're silent, the more curious I am," Blake said, prodding her to confess her naughty thoughts. And judging from the glint in his eyes, he had already guessed they were naughty.

"It really isn't important," she said, swallowing the lump forming in her throat. "Because I'm not making a bet that includes me jumping out of a plane. Besides, we have drinks with Meagan and the crew. There's no time for bets or anything else." Really? Had she really just said "or anything else"? The elevator doors opened. "Home sweet hotel," she said. "I want to change before we meet the others for drinks."

They stepped out into an elegant lobby area of red oriental carpets and impressive artwork. Her nerves tingled just thinking being in a hotel room she'd been fantasizing about for hours—or rather, a hotel room with Blake in it.

She glanced down at her key. "1835."

"I'm next door." He motioned toward the hallway that led to their rooms. "If you want to change, we better get moving."

They started down the hallway, her gaze traveling the luxurious corridor. "Hopefully our bags will arrive quickly." There was a nervous hitch in her voice that Blake couldn't ignore.

"You looked really stunned over the paparazzi issue. You do realize you're about to be a big star, don't you?"

"Don't say that," she chided quickly. "It's bad luck to assume success. And I don't care how popular season one was, season two could tank. Or I could tank. They could decide I'm too young or too old or too fat or too tall. Or I don't resonate with the audience or—"

"Worry much?" he asked her.

She let out a breath. "I excel at it, yes."

"You can't survive this business like that," he said. "You'll drive yourself insane." They stopped in front of her door and he motioned to it. "Just as I promised. I got you to your room safely, without being seen, and without taking advantage of you." He leaned against the door. "But no one said you can't take advantage of me."

Her desire burned a little brighter. "I'm not drunk."

"Are you giving me permission to take advantage of you?"

Blake's words *you can't live like that* resonated with her. She truly was a worrier, and she was about to let that worry cheat her out of a night with Blake. It was now or never.

A hallway door opened and Darla turned away, feeling like a child caught with her hand in the cookie jar. A bellman wheeled their bags forward from what appeared to be a service entrance.

"Saved by the bellman," Blake said, pushing off the wall.

Darla turned back to him, determined to salvage her "now or never" moment. "Who said I wanted to be saved?"

5

DARLA WATCHED HIS DARK EYES, full of understanding and desire. For her. This wasn't about television ratings or competition. It was just about a man and a woman, and she didn't remember the last time she'd let herself experience such a thing. Actually, she wasn't into strangers and casual sex, so she'd never done something like this. But then, Blake wasn't a stranger. Not really.

"Ms. James?" the bellman asked from behind her.

"Yes," she said, turning to greet the young man. "That's me. Thanks for being so quick." She stuck her key in her door.

"I'll just grab my bag myself," Blake told the kid, his attention capturing Darla's for a moment. She thought she might combust from heat if he spent the next few hours looking at her like that. Everyone was bound to notice, too. She gave him a warning glare.

Blake's lips hinted at a lift and his eyes danced with amusement. "Thanks for the promptness," he said to the kid, passing him a tip before he retrieved his bag.

He gestured toward the elevator. "I'll meet you here in twenty minutes, if that works?"

She swallowed hard. "Ah, yes. Sure." Was he serious or...?

He rolled his bag to his door.

Feeling more than a little out of sorts, she forced her attention from Blake and opened her door. The bellman carried her bag inside and she added to his tip. When all was said and done, the kid departed and Darla poked her head into the hallway. Blake was in his room, it appeared, his door firmly shut. She shut her own door and fell back against it. Was he being discreet or...*no!* She refused to believe Blake was playing her. She felt a connection with him, a level of comfort she never felt with another man so quickly, if ever. A knock sounded on the door and she jumped. The knock sounded again. Darla grabbed the door and pulled it open.

Blake stood there, tall and broad, still wearing his faded jeans and T-shirt, looking too sexy for her own good. "You gonna invite me in or leave me out here where someone might see me?"

"I have to get ready for drinks." She looked at her watch. "We have fifteen minutes."

"It was canceled," he said. "Now can I come inside?"

She backed up and let him in, fearful he would be seen and eager for an explanation. "What do you mean drinks are canceled? I didn't get a call."

He stepped inside and shut the door, sliding her lock into place and turning to face her. A mixture of hot man scent and some deliciously right cologne washed over her, overpowering her with a spike in awareness. Of the man. Of the bed behind her—that she wasn't going anywhere near until she knew what was going on.

"Meagan tried to call and text you, but apparently you don't have good reception in the mountains. They've had some security issues at the audition site." He leaned on the door as she had just moments before. "She had to cancel."

"Oh, no," Darla said, obviously alert, concerned. "What kind of security issues? We have to go and help out."

"Wait. There's more." He read from his cell phone. "Blake. When Darla offers to come over and help us— and since I know Darla well, she will—tell her I said no. Sam gets cranky when too many people get involved with his things. I suggest both of you just get some rest and we'll see you in the morning." He glanced up at her.

"My God, she typed you a full memo in text message."

"Yeah, she did," he agreed. "But our bottom line here is that there is no meeting and no drinks with Meagan." He reached for her and pulled her against him, his hand sliding down her back, molding her to his long, hard body. Her thighs pressed to his, her hips melded to his, making the thick ridge of his erection more than evident. "So, instead of a bet," he murmured, "how about we negotiate more of a deal?"

"I'm not sure why that's different but I'm not skydiving." Her hands settled on his chest, his impressively hard chest, and warmth seeped into her palms. She couldn't believe she was doing this, that this was really happening, that she wasn't even trying to talk herself out of it. "Just for the record, if at any point before you leave this room and I tell you I will skydive, don't believe me. I won't be responsible for saying it. If you can live with that, then I want to know what your 'deal' is."

"The idea that I might get you to agree, even if you change your mind later, isn't a bad one." He laughed. "But no skydiving. This is the 'deal.' For the rest of the night, if I can't make you forget to worry about tomorrow morning, then my father will go on your show. I'll give him the thumbs-up to embarrass the hell out of me, and believe me, not only will he do so and do it well, he'll enjoy every second. My father revels in that kind of stuff. But if I succeed, then you give me my interview and we talk about the shoe incident and clear the air in the same public way this war started."

"That's big Texas talk and big Texas demands, if I ever heard them."

His hand traveled a path up her back, to her neck, under her hair. "Sweetheart, talking isn't what I have on my mind." His bent toward her, his mouth a breath from hers, tickling her lips and so much more with promise. "Do we have a deal?"

If it was going to get him to kiss her, and sooner rather than later, oh, yeah, they did. "Sure," she said. "We have a dea—" His mouth closed down on hers before she ever got the final word out.

BLAKE HAD INTENDED TO START slowly with Darla, to start with tender, seductive kisses, before exploring every inch of her sleek, sexy body. Intended but failed. She wrapped her arms around his waist, her lush breasts pressing against his chest. And once again, when he'd have sworn it was no longer possible for a woman to do so, Darla seduced him, not the other way around. The instant Blake had set eyes on her again in the New York airport, and ten times over since, she controlled him without even trying. He was charmed by her, intrigued by her, and he was lost in the touch of her soft, yielding lips beneath his.

He deepened the kiss, his hand caressing her heart-shaped backside, which he'd admired more than a few times during this trip. A delicate, erotic little sound of her pleasure unraveled him, ripping through him like rocket fuel. Fuel for a simmering desire he'd been holding back, since the moment she'd fallen off her broken shoe and into his arms. Hell, he'd not touched another woman since, and now he knew why. He was tired of settling for sating a male urge, rather than truly feeling something beyond simple, short-lived lust. Finally, someone had made him feel something real, something worth staying for, something worth experiencing.

He turned her so that she was against the wall, his legs framing hers, his hands gliding over her waist to her breasts. His teeth scraped her bottom lip. "What are you thinking about?"

"You," she added in a teasing voice, "and tomorrow morning when I begin the biggest career move of my life. So I'd say you still have some work to do to uphold your end of our 'deal.'"

"Now you're just being bad." But dang, he liked it. His gaze held hers, his thumbs brushing over her nipples pebbled against her thin T-shirt. She bit her lip, her face etched with pleasure. "And I'm clearly not doing this bet service if you can mock me so easily."

"I thought it was a deal," she said, "not a bet."

"Deal," he conceded, shoving her shirt upward, then pulling it over her head and tossing it behind him. His gaze fell to her breasts, to the bra that, somehow, so fit her. "I knew it would be pink."

She crinkled her nose at him. "You did not. And if you did, you shouldn't have been thinking of my bra in the first place."

"No?" he asked, pulling it down to tease her pretty rose-colored nipples. "I'll be better next time."

"There won't be a next time," she said breathlessly, her teeth scraping over her bottom lip. "We're competitors. We don't belong in bed together and this is against my better judgment."

He glanced at her. "Yet I'm here."

"We have one night and then we're worlds apart," she agreed. She leaned into him, her hand sliding down his crotch, caressing the hard ridge of his erection. "I wasn't going to let that pass me by, but we better make this count. There's no do-over."

They weren't competitors. Her career was going places he'd long ago decided he didn't want to go, but to tell her that would only remind her of the pressure she was under, and that would defeat the entire purpose of their "deal." "I plan on making it count," he said and placed his hand over hers, over his pulsing erection. "Just as I plan on making you forget anything but how *bad* I can be." He turned her around to face the wall.

"Blake—" The objection died on her tongue as she tried to turn and he stopped her.

"Stay where you're at," he ordered. His hands settled on her waist, his cock against her backside.

"I want—"

"To be in control," he finished for her, leaning into her. He pressed his lips to her ear, even as one hand popped her bra clasp. "And sweetheart, if that's what you want, I'm all yours. But you know what I think?" He slid the bra straps forward until she shrugged out of them, then filled his palms with her breasts, his teeth nibbling her lobe. "You'll overthink what that means. You'll worry that you aren't doing it right. You'll worry that I'm like the studio and wonder if I think you're too young or too old, or too something, when all I'm think-ing—" he turned her back around, wanting her to see the truth in his eyes "—is how damn perfect you are and how damn lucky I am to be with you tonight." And he meant that. This wasn't just about their obvious physical attraction. Somehow he had to show her that.

"Blake." This time his name was a whisper rather than a command, her voice and her lovely features etched with vulnerability.

"Believe me," he said, brushing a silky strand of hair behind her ear, knowing he had to earn her trust. "And, Darla. What happens here stays here. I just want to make sure you know that. This is our time, our experience and our secret." He dipped his head, brushed his mouth over hers. "You have my word." His fingers trailed over her jaw, her neck, over one of her nipples. His gaze swept over her body, then lifted. Their eyes collided, the air sexually charged. One minute they were staring at one another, the next, they were kissing, touching, her soft hands sliding under his shirt, pushing it upward.

Blake tugged it over his head and before he even tossed it away, her mouth was on his chest, her teeth grazing his nipple, her fingers working the button on his jeans. Had any woman ever felt this good? Every inch of his body was aware of her. He wondered what she was thinking, what she was feeling beyond desire.

"No, sweetheart," he groaned, capturing her hand before she worked the zipper down. "Not yet. I want you way too much to rush this, and I'll be damned if I let you get away from me without making sure you remember tonight." And that she would give him a chance for another night, which he was pretty damn sure wasn't going to come easy and he already knew he wanted. She might justify their bedroom adventure as here and gone, but he wouldn't be here if that's what this was, if there wasn't more to this. She pushed to her toes and kissed him, and the instant her tongue touched his, he was a goner. He lost himself in the honey-sweet taste of her, the feel of her skin against his. Quickly, she unzipped his jeans and pressed her hand inside his boxers, her slender fingers wrapping around his shaft. Blake moaned and pulled away from her, squatting to help her take off her boots. He had to slow things down, otherwise it would be a "wham, bam, thank you ma'am" experience that he was certain as Sunday would haunt him the rest of his life.

"Now, where were we?" he said, her boots gone now, and his, too. He ran his hands up her legs as he stood, to settle on her hips. "Oh, yeah. We were talking about how you'd agreed that I'm in control so you can just relax and let me take you away."

"We didn't agree to anything of the sort," she said, swallowing hard as he worked the front of her jeans.

"Pretend." He tugged her jeans down and noticed the blond triangle of neatly trimmed curls that came into view. He glanced down and then up, and playfully tried to put her at ease. "No underwear?"

"I don't like panty lines," she said, stepping out of her pants without hesitation.

"Of course," he said, wrapping his arm around her to comfort her. "I hate panty lines." He gently tweaked her nipples, then soothed them with his thumbs.

"Aren't you the funny man?" There was a breathless quality to her voice that told him he was getting to her, and he liked it. He liked it a lot.

"It's not my intention to be funny," he assured her, kicking her jeans aside. "In fact, why don't I show you just how seriously I'm taking your pleasure right now?" He dropped to one knee, settling his hands on her hips. "Do I seem like I'm trying to be funny?"

She wet her lips. "No. *Funny* isn't the word that comes to mind."

He pressed his lips to her stomach. "Then what word comes to mind?" He kissed her again then ran his tongue around her belly button. Her belly quivered. The vulnerability it showed made his chest expand, tighten. She was like a delicate flower, and a sense of protectiveness toward her surprised him. He didn't want to keep her at a distance, which defied everything he'd taught himself about self-preservation. He glanced up at her, aware she'd yet to reply. "What are you thinking?"

"Am I supposed to be thinking right now?"

He smiled against her stomach, pleased with that answer. If she wasn't thinking, she was letting go; she was trusting. "Not if I can help it." He slid his fingers into the slick heat of her sex, his cock pulsing at the intimate touch.

She made a soft sound, squeezing her thighs around his hand. "We really should move to the bed before I fall down."

"I won't let you fall," he promised, his lips traveling over her soft, silky skin, his teeth grazing her sexy hip bone, the curve of her waist.

"If you keep doing what you're doing," she whispered, "I'm not sure you can stop me."

His fingers delved past the slick folds of her sex. He sought the sweet spot he knew would drive her wild. And he wanted to drive her wild. He wanted to see her let go of her control, to relinquish her prim and proper persona fully—for him, with him. "I want to taste you, Darla." He lifted one of her legs over his shoulder, his fingers explored her more intimately, his thumb flickering over her clit. "Any objection?" He leaned in and licked her clit, glancing up at her, arching a brow.

"You don't really expect me to say 'no,' do you?"

He chuckled, licking her again and again until she gasped and her head fell back against the wall, her dark lashes sweeping her ivory cheeks. Blake suckled her swollen nub, stroking her with his fingers, still seeking that sweet spot that would drive her wild. He knew he'd found it when she moaned deeply and laced her fingers into his hair. The more he licked, the more he delved and stroked and teased, the firmer her fingers tightened on his hair. She rocked her hips, pumping against his fingers. He felt her stiffen, heard her suck in a breath. She went still—and he knew she was on the edge ready to tumble, one lick away from orgasm. He suckled her instead, drawing out her pleasure, then swirled his tongue around her nub. Her hands flattened on the wall a moment before her body jerked, hips lifting against him. Spasms spiraled around his fingers. His body reacted instantly, his cock a hard ridge against his stomach, ready for her the next time she came.

His cell phone started to vibrate on his belt, but he didn't think he'd care if the fire alarm was going off right now. He was too into Darla, too into her honeysuckle-sweet taste, her scent, her perfect ivory body. Her satisfaction. That was the ultimate turn-on, the ultimate goal, and Blake went after it with the fierceness of a wild animal. He wanted it, he had to have it. Nothing but her complete, utter satisfaction would do. And so he licked and caressed her to a simmering slow down until she inhaled deeply, as if she'd forgotten to breathe, and that breath brought her back to reality.

She blinked down at him, her cheeks flushed red, her bottom lip swollen from his kisses. "That was…" she started, her voice trailing off, her teeth working her bottom lip.

"A warm-up," he promised, kissing the inside of her thigh and easing her leg over his shoulder and her foot back to the ground. "We're only just getting started." He pushed to his feet, palming her backside and lifting her.

She made a surprised sound and hung on to him, her arms holding tight around his neck and her legs around his waist. He went down on the bed on top of her, the feel of her beneath him a tiny piece of heaven. "I have to warn you," he confessed, "you've got me right on the edge, sweetheart, and my slow romancing is about to explode into fast and hard if we aren't careful."

"Fast and hard sounds good right now," she said, again proving she wasn't all about prim and proper. "But you said it yourself. Talk is cheap and you're still wearing your pants."

His cell phone vibrated on his belt again and her eyes went wide. "Is that your phone?"

"Yes," he said. "And whoever it is can wait." He slanted his mouth over hers, claiming her. She whimpered, her tongue searching for his, her hands gripping his back. One of her legs entangled his as if she feared he'd get away. He wasn't going anywhere. His phone vibrated again. Ignoring it with Darla underneath him and her hands all over his body wasn't hard. Hell. He couldn't even manage to pull himself away from her long enough to fully undress. She tasted of honey, felt like sunshine.

He spread her legs wider and sank deeper between them. Arching against her sex, his hands explored her body.

"Please," she whispered. "Take off those damn pants before I scream in frustration."

"One more kiss," he said. Just then, the hotel phone started to ring. Blake went still. He burned to kiss her into oblivion and ignore the call, but he couldn't. Not when his phone had been going off and hers wasn't getting a good mountain signal. He was so frustrated, the last thing he wanted was to make her feel second to anybody in that moment. "As much as I don't want you to, you have to get that. It could be the studio." He rolled off her and grabbed his phone, checking his text messages. "It's Meagan. She wants us to meet her for drinks after all."

Darla scrabbled for the nightstand. Blake turned to find her grabbing the phone and giving him an alluring view of her creamy white backside. The one he'd had pressing into his palms a few minutes ago. The one he had a feeling wasn't going to be pressed into his palms again tonight.

"Yes, hi, Meagan," Darla said, sitting up and looking over her shoulder at him. "I'm not sure about Blake. His phone must be having signal issues, too." She frowned. "I'll go knock on his door. Sure. Yes. I'll meet you in twenty minutes." She hung up the phone. "I can't believe this is happening."

Blake grabbed her and pulled her back into his arms. Damn, she felt good, and he didn't want to let her go. "And I can't believe I had you naked and never even managed to get my pants off. You're going to regret this as soon as we leave this room, aren't you?"

"Of course I am," she said, her words giving him an unexpected jab in his chest until she added, "What kind of woman can't get a man's pants off?" She pressed her lips to his. "And now I'm going to be thinking of how to do it the entire time we're with Meagan."

"And even if I buy that, which I don't, I know where this is headed. Our one night just ended."

"Well," she said, barely giving him a pebble of hope. "It could be fast and everyone says good-night."

"More likely," he said unhappily, "it'll stretch into hours when everyone should be in bed resting. Except you. You should be in bed with me."

She laughed. "That was my plan, in case you hadn't noticed." She ran her fingers over his jaw. "Thank you for making sure I didn't miss that call when you could have easily distracted me from it."

He drew her fingers to his lips. "I better leave or I won't let you get dressed." He started to get up.

"Wait." She grabbed his arm. "What if you're seen leaving my room? Sounds like there's show personnel already going. We're competitors, Blake. If my station finds out that we, ah… Well, it could jeopardize my show. The studio might think I have your interests, not theirs, in mind."

"Things would have to go horribly bad for you in all kinds of nearly impossible ways for that to happen, and they won't." She started to object and he held up a hand. "But I understand you're worried and I'll be discreet. Complain about your phone service and tell everyone I stopped by to make sure Meagan was able to reach you. That way, if anyone sees me leave, you have an explanation."

"Right," she said. "Good thinking."

He glanced down at her bare breasts and back up. "I wasn't kidding about not letting you get dressed."

She tugged up the comforter and slid underneath, then smiled. "Go, before I don't let you, and that would be very bad."

"Or very good, depending on how you look at it." She started to object and he leaned in and kissed her. "I'm leaving."

He pushed to his feet and searched for his shirt, finding it in the hallway. He tugged it over his head and quickly put on his boots before hesitating at the door. He didn't want to leave and that said a lot, when he normally couldn't run from a woman's door fast enough. Of course, they'd had a premature finish, but still... he wasn't ready to walk away from Darla. Not until he understood what she was doing to him. He resisted the urge to back up and tell her exactly that, or at least frame a plan to end up here after tonight. Dang it, Darla was making him feel every bit the primal man. Some part of him wanted to declare her "mine." That thought rattled him to the core, and he reached for the door. A cold shower and some stern self-reprimanding were in order—and fast.

6

DARLA SAT ON THE MATTRESS, unsure of what had just happened. He'd left. He'd had no choice. He'd even said he didn't want to leave. But yet, he had, and they'd made no plans for what came next. Did anything come next? Probably it shouldn't. Darla liked Blake. She liked him a lot—too much, in fact. History told her that was trouble, especially with a man who'd been trouble in the past. She shook herself, realizing that she should be showering and dressing, but was thinking about Blake when she should be thinking about her job. Grimacing at the man's ability to distract her, she shoved away the comforter and rushed to the bathroom.

Fifteen minutes later, she'd managed a superfast shower, changed into a clean, dressier pair of jeans and a pale pink blouse. Her hair had been a wild mess, compliments of Blake's hands. But thanks to a hot iron, her hair was now smooth and orderly. Her makeup had been reapplied, the whisker burns covered. His whisker burns—Blake Nelson's whiskers. They had felt really good on about every part of her body. How in the heck was she going to face him in a group of people and act like he hadn't just rocked her world? She didn't want Meagan or anyone else to think she wasn't focused on her job.

She grabbed the small pink beaded purse she'd unpacked, filled it and crossed the strap over her head and shoulder, before making her way to the hallway. Darla glanced at Blake's door. Should she knock? What would she do if the man hadn't just been half-naked with her? That was pretty hard to think through when being naked with him was pretty darn heavy on her mind—so was every flirtatious second leading up to her being naked. But prior to tonight she'd considered him her competitor—even her enemy. Yet she'd bonded with him on the plane and they had become friends. She didn't give herself time to reconsider. Darla rushed to his door and knocked, then nervously looked around. Which was absolutely crazy. They'd flown into town together. They could walk to drinks together. She knocked again, more confidently this time, but he didn't answer. He wasn't in his room. He'd left *without* knocking on her door. Okay. So she wasn't sure what to make of that. The worrier in her could conjure all kinds of trouble that she didn't need right now.

Darla started walking toward the lounge area, her stomach suddenly fluttering with renewed nerves, which she tried to squash. The process of said squashing wasn't going well, and by the time she stood at the door of the lounge, she was worse, not better. But when she entered the room, she realized the show was on. A group of about twelve, maybe even fifteen, of the show's staff sat around a group of tables shoved together in the center of an oval-shaped room. Her gaze moved past the tables, drawn to the ceiling-to-floor windows and the view beyond that, which mesmerized, even calmed, her. The sun and mountains had faded into a pitch-black sky decorated with twinkling stars and city lights.

"Darla!" Meagan called, waving her forward. Her light brown hair fell haphazardly from a pile on top of her head, her jeans and T-shirt were casual and comfortable. The big burly blond man next to Meagan stood, as well, and Darla assumed him to be Meagan's new husband. Evidently, he'd used his role as head of studio security to ensure he was the man watching over his wife and her show. Darla found this endearing and romantic.

Seeing Meagan again dissolved what was left of Darla's nerves. Meagan wasn't a big bad studio person. She might be Darla's new boss, but she was also one of the nicest people she'd ever met. Someone she knew could blossom into a close friend.

Darla rushed forward, and was soon trapped in Meagan's warm hug. "I can't believe you're here." She leaned back. "Isn't it crazy how both of our lives have changed in such a short time?" They'd met during the casting of the first season of the show and quickly bonded. Like Darla, who'd started out in casting and become a camera personality, Meagan had taken an unexpected path, from injured dancer to producer of a reality dance show.

Affection filled Darla and she paused to look at Meagan. "I can't tell you how much it means that you made this happen for me. I'm not going to let you down."

"I know that or you wouldn't be here," Meagan assured her. "I really wanted to make drinks happen so you could meet your fellow judges before the first audition. But before I introduce you to everyone, I have to warn you, Darla, last season, we didn't have anyone but our own crew and a few local press people on hand for the auditions. We couldn't even get a good showing for the contestants. There are people who have been camped out for a full day already. This season is already chaotic but we have plenty of talent this time."

Darla grinned. "I'll be the judge of that." Auditions had gone so poorly last season that Darla had personally set up some additional New York tryouts, where a bulk of the cast had been found.

Meagan grinned back at her. "Exactly why you're here. But consider yourself warned. It's going to be a wild ride the next few weeks."

"She's not kidding," Sam said, offering Darla his hand. "Sam Kellar. Nice to finally meet you, and good thing we did it tonight. Something tells me I'm going to be on duty around the clock from here on out."

"So nice to finally meet you, too," Darla said, accepting his hand. "I guess the security threat is over now?"

He scrubbed his jaw. "We had some contestants get into a fight outside the hotel."

"Needless to say," Meagan added, "those individuals won't be auditioning. I don't like trouble or scandal. I'm trying to keep this show more *American Idol* than

Jersey Shore. After last season, I know all too well that once we start filming the reality portion of the show that's incorporating the contestant house, it'll be a pipe dream to avoid."

Meagan motioned to the chair in front of Darla. "I saved you a seat so we could chat. Let's eat, drink and drink some more—God, don't I wish I could do that, but morning will be here soon enough." Meagan and Sam sat down, and Darla grabbed her chair, looking across the table for the first time. That's when her gaze froze, her eyes colliding with the wicked heat of Blake's sexy blue stare.

"Glad you made it," he said, a twinkle of mischief in his eyes.

"We were starting to worry you might have fallen asleep," Meagan teased. "But Blake said you drank a pot of coffee on the plane."

"I did," Darla said, easing into her chair and wondering what else Blake had said exactly, and from the look on his face he not only knew it, he was enjoying it. "And since I fly horribly, Blake felt the full wrath of me on a caffeine and fear high. But then, he's my competitor, so who better to torture but him?"

Meagan laughed and waved a finger between the two of them. "That's right. You two have a little baggage of your own, don't you?"

"We did," Blake said. "But she forgave me."

Darla crinkled her nose, wondering why she was looking at his mouth. Oh, yeah, she knew why. It had been all over her body, which was a very bad thing to think about right now. "I didn't actually forgive you." Okay, maybe. Almost. If they'd had just a bit longer alone.

"We made a deal, though, Darla, remember?" Blake asked.

Her mouth gaped. "What?" He wouldn't. He couldn't. She'd trusted him, and that meant he probably would.

"Hi, Darla. So good to see you again."

Darla cringed at the greeting and not just because of the timing. She'd already noticed who was sitting on Blake's left and it was all Darla could do to force her gaze from Blake to the source of the greeting. Lana Taylor was the gorgeous, twentysomething Broadway star with trademark long red hair and pale, perfect skin, who was a second season judge. She'd also acted like a mean diva to Darla's staff during a guest spot on her show, post *Stepping Up* season one. Darla wondered if she regretted her behavior now. The world was always smaller than people thought. Then again, Lana was the mean judge on the show—mean just seemed to be a part of her character.

"Hi, Lana," Darla said, leaving off the "nice to see you again" because Darla tried really hard to stay sincere in a business that tended toward the opposite direction. Her gaze drifted back to Blake's, to his clean-shaven jaw. The skin of her stomach and leg tingled where that stubble had grazed her earlier, taunting her with how intimately exposed she was to this man, and this table, if he chose to betray her.

"Nice to meet you, Darla."

Darla inhaled and greeted another judge sitting to Lana's left. Jason Alright was a sexy thirtysomething Vegas producer who'd been a favorite of the viewers' last season, especially with the female audience.

The fourth and final judge was Ellie Campbell, who was about Darla's age and one of the hottest choreographers in the business. Ellie, who had pink hair tonight, was known for frequent, unique hair color choices and hip street-style clothing. She sat at the far end of the table, but quickly appeared at Darla's side to offer a friendly introduction. Darla liked Ellie instantly and as Jason joined the conversation, she found him quite likable, as well. Everyone got along with Blake, she noticed.

A number of crew members chimed their greetings to Darla. There were some friendly, familiar faces Darla was glad to see. And she told herself this distraction was good. There was no time, or room, for Blake to fit in more about their "deal." But she'd fit it in all right. She and Blake were going to have a good heart-to-heart, sooner rather than later.

"I'm so excited to see you again," Lana continued after everyone settled back into their own conversations. "You went from casting to your own show. Impressive, Darla. You're rocking showbiz."

It was a sticky-sweet compliment lacking sincerity and laced with a chill. "And on that note," Darla said, feeling the ball and chain of performance pressure tugging at her, she lifted her hand to flag a waiter. "Can I get a dessert menu?"

"What about dinner?" Blake asked.

She gave him a pointed look. "I have a sudden urge to go straight to the heavy stuff."

"The camera adds ten pounds," Lana sweetly reminded them.

"Good thing tonight will only be worth about a pound of that ten," Darla said, accepting a menu from the waiter. "Because I fully intend to indulge."

"I said it earlier," Blake chimed in. "And I'll say it again. I'm so glad I'm a man. We really don't give a damn about a pound or ten."

He'd changed his shirt to a dark blue collar tee with a studio logo and he wore it like he wore the room—casual and comfortable. He had this cool air of confidence about him that screamed of being comfortable in his own skin, never rattled or out of his element, and she envied him that.

"What did I say that merited an urgent request for dessert?" Lana asked, laughing. "Surely, you aren't nervous. You have a show and an audience of your own."

Darla could play coy and cool with Lana, but that just wasn't her style. "I have a show and an audience," she agreed. "But not a prime time show with millions and millions of viewers. That audience is going to expect this season to be better than the last, and with me being the newbie, I'll be under the microscope."

"And hearing you talk about the viewers wanting this season to be better than the last makes me want a big fat dessert, too," Meagan said, nudging Darla's menu closer so that she could see what was on offer. "I keep thinking that what goes up must come down and we have to get off the ride before it does. Go out gracefully, with style, and on our own terms. And with some reality show kind of twist."

"Hearing you talk about the program ending is only making me more worried," Darla said. "At least your job is secure."

"Oh, please," Meagan pleaded. "You'll be great and everyone will love you."

"We hope," Darla replied. "We both know there is no certainty in this business."

"You two are not good for each other," Blake said, moving a finger between Meagan and Darla and then lifting his chin at Sam. "I just spent hours on a plane with Darla from New York and she freaks herself out enough. Together, it's clear that they are dangerous to each other's sanity."

"And everyone around them," Sam readily agreed.

"We need to have Darla and Lana change seats," Blake suggested, "so there's some distance between Darla and Meagan."

Was he really trying to jockey for her to sit next to him? And did he really think that wasn't obvious? Darla gave Blake an incredulous look and kicked him under the table.

"Ouch!" Lana screamed. "Someone just kicked me." She rubbed her leg. "Who did that?"

Darla's eyes went wide. Blake burst out laughing. Meagan looked between Darla and Blake, then to Lana, and immediately turned to her husband. "Sam," Meagan scolded. "I told you to be careful with those big, long legs of yours."

Oh, thank you, Meagan! But Blake barked more laughter, and the rest of the group was looking their way. Darla considered kicking him again, only she hadn't kicked him in the first place, so for safety's sake, she settled for a glower and a silent promise that she was going to kill him. He laughed louder. "Stop laughing!" Lana ordered Blake. "It hurts."

"I'm so sorry, Lana," Meagan said, squeezing Darla's leg under the table, telling her she knew darn well who had kicked Lana. Meagan eyed her husband. "Sam. Apologize."

"I didn't—" Sam grunted, and Darla had a feeling Sam had just gotten pinched or kicked himself "—mean to," Sam finished. "I didn't mean to kick you, Lana. I'll be more careful. Sorry about that."

Lana scowled at poor Sam. "Remind me not to sit next to you. I'm going to have a giant bruise."

"Yeah," Sam said. "Sorry again." His gaze slid curiously between Blake and Darla. "I think I want to hear about this deal—*ouch*." He grimaced at Meagan. "Would you stop that?"

Darla's heart leaped. She couldn't speak and couldn't breathe for that matter.

The deal was about to be exposed.

7

"DEAL?" BLAKE ASKED IN REPLY to Sam, but his attention stayed on Darla a moment before flickering to the other man. "Did I say deal? I meant truce. Darla has agreed to forgive me for our past 'incident' for the good of the show. Rick is on his own, though. Where is he, by the way?"

"I don't remember saying that I forgave you," Darla said and eyed Meagan. "And yes. Where is Rick? I'm looking forward to giving him a nice warm greeting."

"He's doing a charity baseball game and won't arrive until late tonight," Meagan said and pursed her lips. "And you better behave when he arrives. You promised me you two would play nice."

"Of course," Darla assured her. "I just want to have a little one-on-one chat with him to make sure I don't become the brunt of any more of his attention-grabbing schemes."

"I already tackled that," Meagan promised, lowering her voice. "Rick knows I'm trying to keep this a top-quality talent show, not an extension of a tabloid."

"Which, as Meagan mentioned," Sam added, "is a tough task once you get six young men and women in a contestant house for eight weeks. The cameras are rolling, the hormones are high, and the weekly live competitions and eliminations are always hanging in the air. But Meagan and I learned from last season. We're determined to run things better this year."

"Even if the studio doesn't believe they're better," Meagan commented. "They love scandal because they think it equals ratings when, in reality, it's our ability to appeal to families that gets us powerful advertisers we'd lose in the long run if we tainted our image. It amazes me that the suits are so blinded by short spikes in numbers, rather than the big picture. Yet, they'll cut us in a heartbeat if I let their strategy dominate the show and it fails."

"Back to the topic of Darla and Rick," Blake said. "The press is absolutely going to try and stir up their past conflict. It's what they do—stir the pot. So even if you talked to Rick, they're going to bait him and Darla, and they'll likely make stuff up if that doesn't work."

Meagan sighed. "I assumed as much."

"Yeah, I know, which is why I say I interview Darla and Rick together tomorrow and address the past then, where I can control the outcome. We'll be able to shut down all speculation and rumor because all three of us will be together." Blake gave Darla a quick nod. "I'll cut extra footage that you can use exclusively on your show and some on mine. Then we both win. Everyone wins."

"It's a good plan," Sam agreed quickly. "We then head off at least one story the press will be chasing and maybe stop one headache."

It *was* a good plan, Darla thought, and she actually found herself wondering if she'd wanted an excuse to see him again all along, that tonight had never been about just one night. Good grief, she was so clearly not good at handling men. "How do you feel about the idea?" Meagan asked, studying Darla.

"How do *you* feel about it?" Darla asked.

"I think it's a good idea," Meagan said. "If you're okay with it."

Darla nodded and glanced at Blake. "But I want us to talk to Rick in advance. I want to know what's going to come out of his big mouth before he says it."

"Expected and understood," Blake agreed, gaze raking her face. "Now I just have to convince you to do a full interview on my show before I have to head back to New York."

It felt as if her stomach had done a somersault, which set off all kinds of warning bells. She couldn't risk a bad judgment call—a misstep tonight that might hurt her contract over something that was going nowhere. He clearly had an agenda and she was part of that agenda. His deal had conveniently been made when she'd been distracted. By his hands. His mouth. His body.

She shook off those thoughts, focused on her own agenda—saving her parents' ranch. "You come on my show."

"I'll come on your show, if you come on mine."

"So now we're back to deals, are we?" she challenged without thinking—a behavior he seemed to incite in her—and cringed for what she might have given away.

His lips twitched and he leaned forward, elbows on the table, his voice soft. "Why don't we call it a 'truce with benefits'?"

"Oh, how funny," Lana said. "That's a play on that movie *Friends with Benefits* where Justin Timberlake and Mila Kunis try to keep friendship and sex separate. Never works, by the way. I've tried." She wiggled an eyebrow. "But sounds like fun anyway. How do I sign up?"

This was so turning into a disaster, Darla chided herself. "Fine," she said to Blake, leaving Lana out of the equation. "We'll show-swap, but let's figure out the details later. I'm having trouble thinking past tomorrow right now."

"Maybe talking out the details will get your mind *off* tomorrow," he suggested smoothly, and she knew he wasn't talking about "talking" at all.

"I don't think so." She shook her head. "The night is short and morning is coming early."

"You sure about that?"

"Absolutely." *Not.* But she should be.

The waiter appeared. "Ready to order?"

Meagan wrapped her arm around Darla's shoulders. "You know what I'm thinking? Let's get room service in your room where Sam won't be so we can do the girl-talk thing before the season starts. I've spent time with everyone else. I want to spend some time with you."

Regret filled Darla as "absolutely not" became an

instant "absolutely yes." She was now absolutely certain that there would be no her and Blake tonight. She wanted to finish what they had started—wanted it maybe a little too much.

AN HOUR LATER, DARLA AND Meagan sat in their sweats and sock feet on Darla's bed with a selection of desserts spread out before them.

"I can't believe we have this many to choose from," Darla said, scooping a bite of a brownie covered with hot fudge. She moaned with pleasure. "This might be a ten camera-pound splurge."

"Hmm," Meagan said, digging her fork into a piece of cheesecake. "While I'm never gonna be the diva *some* people associated with the show have become, I do enjoy a splurge here and there." She took a bite and then added, "So…what was up with you and Blake tonight?"

Darla's heart raced and she busied herself with the carrot cake. "What do you mean?"

Meagan gaped. "You tried to kick the man." She snorted. "I died when you kicked Lana. That was hilarious. Lana plays that villainous role well and she eats it up. We all, audience included, love to hate her. If only we could have gotten that on camera."

Darla started laughing. She and Meagan had talked about Lana way back during the casting of season one. "That kick did work out pretty well, but poor Sam. You made him take the rap for me."

Meagan shrugged. "I'll make it up to him later. But

seriously. What's up with you and Blake? I might be married but I'm not blind. The man is easy on the eyes."

Darla stabbed the brownie. "And infuriating, and arrogant, and just so— The man made me want to kick him under the table. That should say it all. He makes me crazy."

"Uh-oh," Meagan said, and grinned. "That's what Sam did to me."

"Oh, no," Darla said quickly. "No. Blake and I are nothing like you and Sam."

Meagan just smiled.

"You don't understand," Darla objected. "I attract all the wrong men. That makes Blake another one of the wrong men."

"Or you choose all the wrong men, like I did," Meagan said, "until the right man steps into your path, like Sam did mine. Then, like Sam also did to me, that right man infuriates you right into love."

Darla shook her head. "I'm not you. Blake is not Sam. And besides, Blake leaves tomorrow." So he wouldn't be infuriating her into bed or into love. *Love*. That was a silly word for her or Meagan to use, one of fairy tales women created over too many drinks or, in this case, too much sugar. She and Blake were oil and water, and people who were oil and water had sex. They did not fall in love.

Meagan just sat there, smiling coyly.

Darla tried again. "Blake and I are not happening. We're competitors. He upsets me. He leaves tomorrow."

Meagan grinned. "Okay."

Frustrated, Darla stabbed the brownie again and took a bite, but she didn't want the brownie. She wanted Blake—which infuriated her all the more. She ate the entire brownie, half the cheesecake and a few bites of several other desserts. And then she blamed Blake for the ten camera-pounds she was going to imagine she had in the morning.

BLAKE DIDN'T THINK MEAGAN would ever leave, but the instant he heard Darla's door open and shut and he knew she'd gone, he dialed Darla's room. Sitting at that lounge table with Darla tonight, he'd done nothing but fall deeper for her. And no, he wasn't going to her room tonight, he knew that. Not because he doubted she would let him, but because he wanted to so damn bad. Because that meant something, and he'd decided she interested him far more than would last one night.

"Hello?" she said in that soft, ever-feminine voice, her tone making it more of a question than a greeting.

"How was dessert?" he asked, lying back on his pillow.

"Better without dodging your bullets at the table," she said. "What's with the 'deal' talk and the 'truce with benefits'?"

"If I'd have known it would have gotten me kicked," he said, chuckling, "I would have controlled myself."

"So not true," she accused. "The 'truce with benefits' comment came after I tried to kick you."

"So you admit you tried to kick me then?"

"Absolutely."

"You're big on the 'absolutely' statements tonight."

"You bet I am. You do remember Meagan saying she didn't like scandal, right?"

"It's only a scandal if someone else knows about it, and they won't."

"We could have been seen," she said. "I shouldn't have taken a risk that we might be seen together."

"Translation. I'm absolutely not coming over tonight, am I?"

"Not a chance."

"Ouch," he said. "I wasn't coming over anyway."

"Good."

"Good, huh?"

"Yeah. Good."

"You aren't going to ask why I wasn't planning to come over?"

"No."

"First of all, you have a big show tomorrow and you need sleep. If I come over, you won't sleep, and then if things go wrong tomorrow you'll blame me. They won't go badly, by the way. You're going to rock the house. But the bottom line is that you doing well matters to me, which brings me to the second reason why I wasn't planning to come over. I *want* to come over. And by that I mean I want to come over more than I should. Too much, Darla."

Silence, until she said, "I don't know what that means."

His voice lowered to meet hers. "Yes. You do." More silence. Okay. That wasn't good. Or maybe it was.

"I have no interest in being in tabloid headlines,"

she said. "That's not how you build a lasting career. At least, not the kind of career I'm building. Not the kind of career I want."

"It's not the kind of career I want, either, and my actions both past and present support that as accurate."

"Tonight, you—"

"Got carried away. You're adorable when you're feisty and I couldn't resist teasing you. But I would never have gone too far. What happens between us, Darla, is between us. I told you that earlier and I meant it."

"Blake—"

"Go to sleep. You have an early morning. I'll see you then." He hung up and then sat there, half expecting the phone to ring again, *wanting* it to ring again. But it didn't. She didn't call back and he had a bad feeling she was far more happy he was leaving tomorrow than he was. Which was exactly why he should go home and not look back. He wouldn't, though. This was new territory for him, that his younger, very happily married brother would find amusing. Blake wasn't laughing but he wasn't running, either. And he had to figure out why, even if that meant taking a few darts from Darla in the process. Hopefully, he could convince her to lick the wounds.

8

YOU KNOW WHAT I MEAN. MORNING came with Blake's words repeating in Darla's head. *And no.* No, she did not *know what he meant,* but she'd darn sure spent the entire night trying to figure it out. No wonder she didn't have one-night stands. Apparently, she was really really bad at them—hauntingly so. She managed to spend the night in bed with the man and he wasn't even there. Darla just hoped she didn't fail the awkward morning greeting as bad, because she was about to see him again.

With that thought in mind, dressed again in sweats, with no makeup on, and her hair freshly washed for a stylist to work magic on, she dragged herself to her door. She'd see *him* on the 6:00 a.m. shuttle to the audition site and she looked like crap—and why, *why* did she care about seeing him, or that she was seeing him premakeup artist? She supposed her distraction meant that Blake had actually achieved success with his "deal" because she wasn't thinking about camera nerves anymore. She'd been thinking of him then, as she was now.

Darla shoved open the door and tugged her roller bag filled with clothing and a variety of other items behind her. The door slammed on the bag and she turned to free it. That was when the door to her left—Blake's door—opened and she stopped.

"Trouble already?" he asked, rushing forward to shove her door open and free her suitcase.

"Yes," she whispered furiously. "And you're it. If you were going to keep me up all night you could have at least done it in person." She wasn't sure who was more stunned by those words—her or him. She froze. He froze. Silence expanded until she finally said, "I can't believe I just said that. More proof that you are making me crazy."

He pulled her suitcase into the hallway and let her door fall shut. He was wearing faded jeans and a T-shirt with *Stepping Up* written on it in a deep blue that matched his eyes. He looked good. So very good.

"*I'm* making you crazy?" he asked, turning the full force of those eyes—those wickedly beautiful eyes—on her.

Darla silently declared it official. Every time he was near, without any effort he got her hot. "Yes. My God. Yes. You are making me crazy. You already know I'm a worrier, a fretter and an overthinker." She'd come this far, she might as well go all the way. "Did you really think you could make a statement like 'you know what I mean' when I didn't know what you meant, and I'd actually sleep?"

"You knew—*you know*—what I meant."

"I *do not* know what you meant and I don't—"

He leaned in and brushed his lips over hers. "Now do you know what I meant?"

Heat spiraled through the center of her body and spread like a wildfire. "Are you insane? Someone could have seen you." But she didn't pull away from him. She should have. She told herself to, but he smelled so darn good—all freshly showered and masculine.

"If that's your only concern about me kissing you then you definitely know what I meant last night. And if you spent the night thinking about it—you definitely knew what I meant. My question is—how do you feel about it?"

Out of control. "We can't do this."

"But you want to?"

"We *can't* do this," she repeated.

"Why not?"

Why not? There were reasons. Lots of reasons. None of them seemed to come to mind. "You like questions, don't you?"

"I'm a television host. Of course, I do. Talk to me, Darla."

A million replies flew through her mind at once, things she'd said already, things she hadn't. *Because you're my competitor. Because you scare the heck out of me for reasons I don't want to think about right now. Because you'll make me care about you and then you'll hurt me.* Finally she said, "You leave today."

"We both live in New York."

"I won't be there for months."

"You'll be back, and I'm not afraid of flying, not to mention you'll have several weeks off when the filming moves to the contestants' house."

"Only for two weeks and not for two months. Which doesn't matter anyway. This was supposed to be…" *A one-night stand.* She couldn't say it out loud despite the wild hair that had made her bold a few moments before.

"I know what it was supposed to be, but it wasn't and it's not. It was never going to be, if we're both honest with ourselves."

She suddenly knew what he'd meant when he said he wanted to come to her room "too much." She liked him too much. Too much for all kinds of reasons. Namely, that no matter how much she didn't want him to be her competitor, or the wrong guy she made the right guy, she really had no control over either thing. No control was bad when she was headed to the first day of a big career move that not only terrified her as much as he did, but meant as much to her family as it did to her.

"No. No. This is bad. This——" she waved a finger between them "——is not smart." She grabbed her bag and tried to move around him. It caught on something, her own foot probably. She stumbled and fell forward and, once again, smack into Blake, just as she had done on the red carpet. His strong hands went to her elbows, his long, hard body catching hers. The concern in his blue eyes stirred a tidal wave inside her. She wanted this man in a bad way, but it was so much more than that. There was this warm feeling in her chest that seemed to expand and do funny things to her stomach.

"It appears the universe is conspiring to throw you into my arms," he suggested. "Maybe you should listen."

The door across from them opened. "I guess I know what 'truce with benefits' means," came a female voice.

Lana. The warm spot in Darla's chest turned to ice. "It appears," Darla said, replying to Blake, "that the universe has a wicked sense of humor."

Darla pushed out of Blake's arms, and with no plan, turned to face Lana. She wore a black sweatsuit, her red hair falling in contrasting silky waves around her shoulders. She wore no makeup and she looked fabulous. Darla wilted, unable to find her voice.

Blake came to the rescue, quickly explaining away their behavior. "The only 'benefits' being received this early in the morning are my personal baggage boy services." He grabbed Darla's suitcase and walked toward Lana, who had one as well, and motioned to her to hand it over. "I'll take yours, too. You can both thank me by not giving me a hard time on camera later."

Lana's lips lifted, and Darla couldn't help but envy how pink and perfect they were. "There's nothing wrong with a scandal," she said. "It's good for ratings. In fact, it's job security."

"Meagan hates scandal," Darla warned. "You have to know that."

"And the studio likes ratings," Lana assured her, making Darla's argument irrelevant. She scooted her bag in Blake's direction. "I do love a man with muscle and manners."

Ratings. Darla heard that familiar bad word with shattering clarity. Lana was going to turn this into ratings, and say to hell with Meagan. Darla knew Meagan trusted her to help maintain a certain image for the show. She didn't want to be the ratings boost—at least, not like this. She had to say something, do something. Fix this.

"My father," Blake said, speaking up in what Darla hoped might be that "fix" because she really had nothing of her own, "raised a scandal-free gentleman. He taught me that a good man carries a lady's bag, holds doors and generally uses good manners. Most importantly, he taught me that a gentleman keeps his private life private. Exactly why I keep my attention, and camera, keenly focused accordingly."

In other words, Darla thought, reading between the lines, Blake wouldn't be giving Lana any feature on his show if she burned him. Darla was thrilled. This was a perfect "fix."

Blake turned to Darla, his eyes lighting on hers as he added, "And a gentleman always catches a lady when she falls."

"I'm pretty sure you're to blame for both of my falls," Darla accused in jest, trying to play off his comment so that Lana wouldn't pick up on the obvious deeper meaning. "The only two times I've stood close to this man, I've tripped over his big feet."

"Oh, I see," Blake said, motioning them all forward. "Is that how it is? It's my big feet, not your clumsiness?"

Darla fell into step with him at the same time that Lana did. "I'm only clumsy when your big feet are in the way." Her shoe caught on the carpet in that instant and she tripped, stumbling and barely catching her footing. She righted herself and ignored Lana, who most certainly was laughing. Her attention flashed to Blake and her gaze found his, they both burst into laughter at the same time.

"Okay fine," she admitted. "I'm not the most graceful person on the planet, but that only makes standing next to those big feet of yours all the more dangerous." There was a lot about him that was dangerous.

Lana punched the elevator button. "Big feet, big—"

"Lana!" Darla objected, appalled she was going there.

"I guess I do have big feet," Blake agreed.

"Neither of you are funny," Darla said, heading into the elevator. Blake joined her, standing beside her, the suitcases parked in front of him. When his arm pressed against hers, Darla felt that one small connection like an electric charge that spread through her entire body. Lana stepped to Blake's other side. Darla turned to rest against the side wall, facing them both. Blake's lips twitched and she knew he knew why she'd moved.

Lana settled against the wall across from Darla. Her gaze slid to Blake and then back to Darla and her lips twisted in an evil little smile. "You really are going to have to lighten up to be on this show. Actually. No. Maybe you don't. I think you might amuse the viewers."

"Amuse the viewers?" Darla asked, feeling like she'd just been insulted. "What exactly does that mean?"

"Your response defines what I mean," Lana replied in an amused tone.

Darla never got the chance to respond. The elevator

doors opened and Jimmy Davis, one of Meagan's production assistants, stood waiting for them.

He flipped his cell phone shut and threw his arms in the air. "Thank goodness." He hit the mic peeking from his mop of blond hair. "They're here." He focused on Darla, Blake and Lana as they exited the elevator. Tall and thin, he was dressed in jeans and a tee that looked like they'd been crumpled by his suitcase. "Damnable mountains in combination with the hotel tower is making cell service impossible. We're doing makeup here. It's just too much of a madhouse at the audition locale." He motioned them forward and Darla and Lana scrambled toward him. Behind her, Darla heard him add, "Blake, stay. You're going down to the garage. We'll take the suitcases, which I assume are the ladies'. Meagan has a situation. She needs you over there with her, as in yesterday. We have a car waiting."

Darla turned to find another crew member retrieving the bags from Blake. "What situation?" Darla asked. "What's happening?"

Jimmy made a shooing motion. "What's happening is you're going that way to makeup. Go, go, go!" Another crew member appeared, a young girl Darla had never met. "Follow Allison."

Darla drew in a breath. Lana shrugged and fell into step behind Allison. The elevator doors shut and Blake was gone with so much unsaid between them, so much unclear.

Jimmy grimaced at Darla. "Please, Darla. I need you out of the main lobby, where we might draw attention."

Darla quickly tried to catch up with Lana and Allison. To say that she was frazzled was an understatement. She was pretty sure Lana believed that she and Blake had a thing going on. But even if she didn't, Darla's gut warned her that Lana would use the possibility as a publicity stunt. Maybe not now, but at some point. Darla had put herself in this spot, starting something with Blake, against her usual good sense. Worse, though, was the out-of-character fact that where Blake was concerned, Darla wasn't sure she had any good sense left to draw on. If she had the chance to hop right back in his arms, regardless of outcome, she all but knew she'd do it. Which made the fact that he was leaving tonight very good. Right. It was a good thing. Her insurance that she would stay out of trouble—the sexy, tempting, really wonderful trouble also known as Blake Nelson.

THE DRIVE TO THE AUDITION location should have been short, but a road was shut off to accommodate the mixture of contestants waiting to perform and fans hoping to see the celebrity judges. The delay gave Blake time to replay that moment when Darla had stumbled in the hallway, then laughed at herself with him. She'd charmed him then—and ten times over. Charmed him, and taken her sex appeal up yet another notch. That every single thing she did was sexy to him told him this wasn't about sex at all. He was pretty sure she could have the flu and be red-nosed and he'd think she was sexy.

The car rounded a corner and Blake couldn't believe his eyes. He sat up, taking in the sight before him. "Holy

smokes," he murmured. There were people and cars everywhere. It was pure mayhem, just as Meagan had said
it had been the prior day. He was about to be out there
in that mess, interviewing people. Adrenaline pumped
through him. He loved everything about the scene—
the wild crowds, the energy. That's why he enjoyed red
carpet events. It wasn't about the stars. It was about the
people who came to see them. His studio audiences were
important to him. They were what was real, what made
him enjoy his work—not the cameras. Like Darla, he
thought. She was real. No fluff and stuff. Ambitious, but
determined to build a strong career with talent and hard
work. Not some get-rich-and-famous publicity scheme.
That was rare in this biz. Rare indeed.

A few minutes later, Blake stepped out of the car in
the private garage to find Meagan waiting for him. "We
have a problem. Or I have a problem. Rick broke his arm
in the charity baseball game."

"And?"

"As in broke it to the point of emergency surgery that
didn't go well."

"That's awful."

"He'll be all right, but in the meantime we want you
to fill in for Rick on the next few shows, until we figure out what comes next. Do this for me, and I'll make
sure the job is yours, if you want it."

Blake was stunned. "My agent—"

"Is waiting for your call. I faxed him the contract. I
know this is short notice. We'll accommodate footage
for your show now and as needed, and we'll get you a

flight home in between this audition show and the one we film Wednesday to take care of whatever you need to take care of."

Blake had always believed that things that fell in your lap were meant to be—just as he was beginning to believe that the lady who had fallen into his arms was meant to be, as well.

A slow smile slid onto Blake's lips. "Count me in."

9

ALL THREE OF THE FEMALE JUDGES, Darla included, sat in chairs lined up inside a small changing room. And all three female judges were receiving the same beautifying treatment. Jason leaned against the wall, one boot pressed to the wall, looking biker bad-boy hot in a way that assured him female audience approval. He'd proven that as a season one judge, but she doubted he cared. He was a famous director. This show wouldn't make or break him. But it could her. Which only made Darla worry about her own audience approval. She forced the thought away and went back to thinking about Blake, which was better than thinking about how important her performance was today. She didn't know where they stood. What if Blake left before she got a chance to say goodbye? Alone, that was. If that happened, would that mean that they were officially "off" or that they were still maybe "on"? She'd told him they were off, so surely that would mean they were off. The entire thing between them felt in limbo and incomplete. "Okay, folks," Jimmy said, rushing into the room. "Let's review our schedule."

While Jimmy paced and talked, Darla's nerves preyed on her. This was it. This was really happening. She was really about to be on one of the hottest shows on television.

"When we get to the hotel," Jimmy said, pausing to look at the four of them, "you'll be taking publicity shots as a group. We'll have the first gang of auditions already inside the building, being prescreened. Once you finish pictures, you'll head straight into the audition room. We're beginning at exactly nine, with cameras rolling. We'll end at precisely seven tonight."

"What exactly was the crisis Meagan had that required Blake's help?" Darla asked. "Is this something that we need to know about before we get there?"

"My job is to worry," Jimmy said. "*Your* job is to be a star and pick stars." He touched his headset. "Yes. Right. Coming now." He glanced at Darla, then his watch, and then, already headed to the door, called over his shoulder, "We leave in fifteen minutes."

"That man gets so hyper," Ellie said from the chair where she sat next to Darla, whose pink hair now glistened with the same kind of tiny purple stones she wore on her jeans.

"That might be the only thing we agree on today," Lana said, standing up to run her hand over her slim-fitting red dress that hit above the knee, her black boots accentuated her long legs. She looked every bit the acclaimed Broadway star. How would Darla live up to that?

"All done," the stylist said, tearing away the cover over Darla's own attire—black jeans with cool floral stitching down the sides and a turquoise V-neck tank. She'd loved this outfit days ago when she'd picked it, but not so much now. Now, she felt like the boring schoolteacher in the midst of rock stars. She felt comfortable on her show and her audience was warm and responsive, her staff, too. They all made her feel like she belonged. Now, though, she wondered how she'd ever gotten here. How she'd ever gotten her own show. She was nothing like these people. She was just Darla from Colorado. How was she ever going to impress viewers and keep her place on the show?

TWENTY MINUTES LATER, they were loaded into a limo—Darla and Ellie on one side and Jason and Lana on the other—about to make a grand front-door entrance to the auditions for the crowd with cameras rolling.

"Isn't it exciting?" Ellie asked, grabbing Darla's arm, clearly thrilled about the lines of people they were passing. "We've come a long way, baby, from last year."

"She's excitable," Lana said, rolling her eyes at Ellie. "Everything is 'exciting.' You'll get use to it."

"Lana's a bitch," Jason said drily. "You'll get use to it." He glanced at Darla. "She'll eat you alive if you let her. Don't."

That statement had Darla stiffening her spine and questioning how she was coming off. "I'm nervous," Darla admitted. "Extremely so. But I'm not a pushover—

especially when it comes to making people's dreams come true."

"We can see you're nervous," Jason said. "You look a little like you might be sick." He motioned toward Lana. "Aim to my right."

"Yes, please," Ellie agreed. "Right before we get out of the limo." She grabbed her phone and seemed to be setting her camera. "I want personal pictures."

"Oh, aren't you funny, Ellie," Lana said, wrapping her arm around Jason and peering up at him. "I guess I better stay nice and close to you so you're in the target range, too." She cut a look at Darla. "And we'll see about that pushover comment. We'll see today, in fact. This should be fun."

Oh, great. Darla, aka the new fish in the pond, had just managed to taunt the resident shark. If things were different, if this job weren't so important to her, she wouldn't care. She'd focus on casting, which she knew she was good at. But things were different, and this was going to be an interesting day. One of many, it was beginning to seem.

"We're here!" Ellie announced. "Lights, camera, action. The new season has arrived."

The car stopped in front of the hotel entrance and Darla could indeed see flashing camera lights. Adrenaline rushed through her. She inhaled and closed her eyes, forcing herself into performance mode, into the place she didn't let the rest of the world bleed into. Where she was a talk show host and no fears could touch her.

But everything happened so fast. The car stopped

and then she was outside, the crowds shouting and calling to her. Darla waved and smiled, blinking against the camera flashes.

Almost the very instant that she and the other judges cleared the front door, they were herded into a room with a big *Stepping Up* panel set up as a backdrop for photos. Blake was there, speaking into the camera, doing an intro about the judges arriving.

Darla's eyes met his for an unintentional instant that both made her heart flutter and made it clear that he was asking several silent questions. Did she want him to stop her, to interview her? She gave a discreet shake of her head. She didn't want to create more speculation about the two of them or risk Lana getting jealous over the camera time.

Blake gave an equally discreet nod and stepped toward Ellie. "Ellie, can you give me a quick sixty-second remark for the camera?"

Darla took a spot in front of the panel that Lana and Jason were already standing in front of, thinking that only a day ago, she would never have thought Blake would be so considerate of her wishes.

"Ellie!" the photographer, a young, spiky-haired, punk-rocker-looking dude, shouted. "I need you in front of my camera, not his." Clearly, the photographer either knew Ellie, or he was just plain cranky in general. Ellie ignored him and kept talking to Blake, which escalated the photographer's demand. "Ellie! I only have a few minutes and I'm good, honey, but even I need everyone in front of the camera."

Ellie grimaced and turned toward him. "Take a chill pill, Frankie, will ya? We're filming and we'll be here all day."

"You might be, but I won't," he assured her. "I have another shoot I'm flying out to in two hours. So unless you want to be excluded from these promo shots, get your butt over here."

"Well, why didn't you say something?" Ellie objected, making fast tracks to join them.

Frankie threw his hands in the air and muttered, "Right. Why didn't I say something?" He flagged Jimmy. "I need Meagan and Rick in ten minutes." He turned back to the group and spoke to one of his assistants, who arranged Darla and the other judges like flowers in a vase. Darla, then Ellie, then Lana, with Jason positioned behind them to offset his six foot-plus height. Frankie fired off a good two dozen camera shots, and then glanced around the room, waving a hand in Jimmy's direction. "We need Meagan and Rick here now."

"Meagan," Jimmy said, rushing forward as he punched his headset and spoke into it. "You're late. We need you here now or we can't get the—"

"I'm here!" Meagan yelled, rushing into the room, clearly flustered. Darla noted Meagan's white jeans and white *Stepping Up* shirt. Meagan's casual attire was a reality check for Darla. She was making herself insane, obsessing over the craziest things, like clothing, when the rest of the judges weren't even dressed up. Evidently, the pressure was getting to her more than she'd realized.

"We have one of two," the photographer complained. "Where's Rick?"

Rick. Darla heard the name and was glad for it. She was really ready to get on with the auditions and the kids with their dreams. She loved casting. She loved that this show let her toe that water again.

"Rick isn't coming," Meagan announced. "He had an emergency and he won't be here today at all." She turned and called out, "Blake! We need you for photos. Hop on over here."

Blake? Darla thought. Why would Blake be in the photos?

"Why is Blake in the photos?" Lana asked, thinking the same thing.

"I'm supposed to have Rick in the shots," the photographer corrected quickly. "I don't see anything about Blake."

"Blake is filling in for Rick," Meagan explained. "I need promo shots for the first show. I want Blake in these shots." She glanced at the group. "And before you ask, I have ideas to spin this Blake and Rick switch-up for ratings. That's all I'm at liberty to say now."

Blake stepped to the side of the set, to Darla's direct right. "You sure about this, Meagan?" he asked, looking as puzzled as the rest of the group.

"Absolutely," Meagan said, using the same word Darla had earlier with Blake. "Details will be discussed when I don't have a thousand people waiting on us outside a hotel." Blake glanced at Darla and then back to Meagan. "The women on this show sure like that word." He shrugged. "I'm easy. I can go with the flow. Where do you want me?"

Frankie motioned to Blake, "Next to Jason."

Blake headed toward the group. Darla quickly turned away, afraid her desire for this man was written all over her face. He stepped behind her and her nostrils flared with the scent of him, warm and spicy, so richly male, so familiar. His hand slid discreetly to her waist and she barely contained a gasp of surprise at what most would consider a casual touch, a posing stance. No different from the way Jason had his arm draped over Ellie's shoulders. Darla knew, though, that Blake's touch wasn't any more casual than the desire sizzling through her.

Meagan rushed forward and squeezed in between Darla and Ellie. She leaned into Darla and touched her head to hers. The camera flashed. "How you doing, sweetie?" Meagan whispered.

"I'm good," she replied softly as more flashes went off. "What's going on with Rick?"

"Surgery for a broken arm," she explained. "He hasn't even made it to Colorado yet."

"You're kidding?" Darla asked Meagan. "Will he make the next show?"

"Face the camera!" the photographer yelled.

"Oh, ah, sorry," Darla said and quickly posed.

The photo shoot wrapped and Darla and the judges headed to the audition room. "Darla," Blake said, gently touching her arm to get her attention before she could get away. She swallowed hard at the impact of those piercing blue eyes that never seemed to lessen. "Don't think about the camera or pleasing an audience," he said, his voice a caress for her ears only. "This isn't live and the auditions won't even be shown for another six weeks. Think about the contestants, about doing what you did last season, and picking the best contestants. Forget everything else or you're going to make yourself crazy."

Darla softened inside, surprised by his words. So very right. "That was *absolutely* what I needed to hear right now." Someone called her name, and she backed away, hesitating to leave, wanting him to know... There seemed to be something she needed to say. She heard her name shouted again.

"Thank you, Blake." Darla rushed away, but silently vowed not to let him leave tonight without a proper goodbye. She was smiling, rather than fretting, when she walked into the audition room.

FOUR HOURS AFTER THE AUDITIONS started, Blake finished an interview with a joyful, crying seventeen-year-old girl who was chosen for the finals. She was the last candidate for now. During the next hour and a half, there'd be prescreening of candidates while the judges were given a chance to eat and take a break.

Beaming at the excitement of the girl and her family, Blake decided he loved this job, and he planned to tell his agent just how much.

Seeking Meagan, Blake stepped inside a small room where the cameras were recording the action in the audition room. Meagan stood in front of a row of monitors, watching the live feed from the judges as it played on the screens.

"Why must you ask every contestant about their dreams and goals?" Lana demanded of Darla. "We simply need them to dance well."

"We're looking for stars," Darla said. "People who have drive and ambition. There's a reason why Jason is so respected in the industry, why Ellie is in demand by big-named stars to choreograph. They're special."

"She's right," Ellie said. "I like hearing people's stories. I've worked with a lot of talent. The ones who make it have certain qualities."

"Hear them after we see them dance, and once they make it to Vegas," Lana argued. "We have a huge line of people out there and not enough time to see them all."

"That's why Meagan has a team of screeners making sure we only see the best," Ellie argued. "The ones we see can dance. But can they become success stories? That's up to us to decide."

"If we send them to Vegas and they have no personality or career potential," Darla added, "then we've wasted time and money. The top twelve are going to be living in the contestant house with a live camera on them. We have to pick people who can become reality television stars or people won't tune in."

"We did fine last season," Lana said tightly. "You need to respect what worked."

Darla drew in a long breath and Blake could see her biting back words. "Tell her," he said softly, stepping to

Meagan's side. "Tell her you cast the winner of last season and most of the top twelve."

Meagan glanced at him, then back at the screen, seemingly waiting right along with him. But Darla didn't tell her. She stood up and said, "We'll have to continue this argument later. I need to check in with my producer back home and make arrangements for filming my show."

Blake scrubbed his jaw. "I don't get it. She'd never let me get away with that. Why didn't she tell her she was the primary casting agent last season?"

"I don't know," Meagan said, still watching the screen. "Her confidence isn't where it normally is. Something is up with her." She glanced at him. "You got anything to do with that?"

"Me?" he asked. "How would I have anything to do with it?"

"You tell me."

He opened his mouth to deny his guilt but shut it again, remembering the incident with Lana in the hallway. Surely, Darla wasn't so worried about a scandal created by Lana's big mouth that she was afraid to stand her ground with her. Then again, he wasn't sure what was behind it, but Darla was almost irrationally worried about losing this job before she even got started. Especially so, considering her own show's success. He wanted to know why. He wanted to know a lot of things about Darla—and not just what made her moan and sigh. Those things were high on his list, but so was discovering what made her happy and sad, what made her afraid of flying. Hell. He wanted to know what her favorite food was. Actually, he was pretty sure that would be chocolate.

Blake watched the screen as Darla walked toward a door that led to a private hallway, and he felt himself stir inside. This woman got to him in a big way and the last thing he wanted to do was create turmoil for her. But he couldn't step back from her without knowing what she was doing to him.

"What's her cell number?" he asked, grabbing his phone from his belt.

Meagan considered him a moment and then recited the number by heart. He was already turning away and hitting the call button by the time she said the last digit. Darla answered almost instantly. "We need to talk and we haven't got long," Blake said. "It's important. I'm about to be at the other hotel waiting on you. *By your door.*" He hung up before she could decline, cringing as he thought of just how mad he'd probably just made her.

He was going to have to do some fast talking to get on her good side.

10

BLAKE QUICKLY LEARNED THAT *MAD* wasn't quite a strong enough word to describe Darla's reaction to his maneuvering her to meet him. She rounded the corner of the bank of elevators, found him by her door, and hit him with a look that could have flattened the entire building. Her cheeks were flushed, her spine stiff, and her eyes as sharp as knives. She stormed towards him, her room key in hand, and she didn't say a word as she stepped next to him to swipe it. He could smell the floral scent of her perfume—jasmine, he thought—and taste her anger. He could feel his desire building at a fairly inappropriate time, for a completely inappropriate reason. She turned him on when she was hot and fiery. She *was* hot and fiery, and she'd shown none of that in that audition room with Lana.

She rushed inside and grabbed his shirt, pulling him with her. His body reacted to the touch, his cock pressing against his zipper. Damn, when had he ever wanted a woman this badly?

"Are you freaking nuts? What kind of stunt are you trying to pull? I didn't sign up for this, Blake. Someone could have seen you. Someone *might have* seen you!"

Blake's plans to talk went right out the proverbial window, his desire for Darla getting the best of him. "Yes," he said, backing her against the door, his legs framing hers and his hands twining into her hair. "I am nuts. Nuts about you."

"Blake," she hissed, splaying her delicate fingers over his chest, scorching him with heat that set his heart to pumping. "I'm furious with you. Don't you understand?"

"I get that," he murmured, lowering his lips to a whisper above hers. "It appears it turns me on. So much so that I'm quickly forgetting I came here to talk." His mouth met hers, claiming the kiss he wanted. She didn't respond immediately—her body was rigid and her hand still flat on the solid wall of his chest. But she didn't push him away and there was just a hint of a moan sliding from her mouth to his.

Blake caressed a palm over her backside. His tongue gently coaxed hers into responding, just a little kiss, a little moment of escape.

"Damn it, Blake," she said gently. Then her tiny moan became a full-out sound of pleasure and her body relaxed into his. The hand resting on his chest traveled upward and wrapped around his neck, the other around his waist. Her tongue caught his, hot and sweet, and eager. He melded her closer, absorbing all her soft curves into his hard body. And he was hard. So hard it hurt to even think about leaving this room without finding his way inside her. She moaned again, her arms wrapping around him, as if she couldn't get close enough. And she couldn't. Not in his book. "This doesn't mean I'm not furious with you," she promised. "It just means that—"

"I know," he said, his cock pulsing thickly against his zipper. "I want you, too." He kissed her and, this time, he didn't even try to hold back. His tongue plunged into her mouth, taking it, claiming it. Claiming her. A taste of honey among the bitterness he hadn't even realized had been eating him alive. This business had gotten to him—the people, the wants, the demands of money and fame. Darla had broken through all of that and she hadn't even tried. She was just herself—and that was unique in his world.

He reached under the silk of her tank, pulled down her bra and fingered her nipples. She shuddered with pleasure, her nails digging into his shoulders. He pushed the shirt upward. "Take it off before I get impatient and ruin it."

She tugged it over her head, leaving her with only her pale pink bra and rose-tipped nipples peeking out. "We can't be late back to set."

"We won't be," he promised, unhooking the front clasp of her bra. "Hard and fast." He teased her nipples, sucking them lightly. "But next time we're going slow and hot. You have my word."

Her hand went to his zipper, tracing his throbbing erection. "Who says there's going to be a next time?" She unsnapped his jeans and the next thing he knew she had her hand on his cock.

He groaned, both from her touch and the way she challenged him. Lust jolted him. He pressed his hand to the wall above her head. "There's going to be a next time. You can count on me doing whatever is necessary to convince you of that fact."

She massaged his shaft, her fingers trailing along the top, spreading the dampness gathering there. "Not if you manipulate me to get me to my room, or anywhere else, ever again."

"We needed to talk," he defended. "And you wouldn't have come any other way."

"Your talking isn't a good idea," she warned, pressing his boxers out of the way and freeing his cock. It jutted forward, thick and pulsing, and she lowered her lashes, inspecting him, stroking him, driving him freaking wild, before her gaze lifted. "Talking is just going to make me mad again. And before you say you like me mad, you should know that mad may or may not include me kicking you out of my room." She slowed her movements, then sped up again.

He barely contained a groan. It felt as if liquid fire was burning through his veins. "Though I do think you're insanely hot when you're mad, I sure as hell don't want to get kicked out of the room right now." He closed his hand around hers. "Keep touching me just like that and I'll shut up." He moved against their joined hands. Her lashes lowered again, her attention on his cock, her tongue biting her bottom lip. It was official. She still hated him and was tormenting him to death. Death by lust. She stroked him harder, faster, and he quickly realized he was further gone than he thought. Too far gone to have her touching him like this if he was going to last—and that sure wouldn't get him a take two. And he wanted a take two, three and four—and whatever and wherever that led. He *wanted* this woman in his life. But he couldn't convince her by pushing her. Not now, at least.

He brought her to the foot of the bed and held her tight, pressing his lips to hers, her bare breasts teasing his chest. He would convince her with pleasure. The kind two people who felt something special for each other could make. "You have on too many clothes."

"So do you," she murmured just before his mouth came down on hers in a searing kiss that burned with a possessiveness so new to him, it threatened to unravel any control he still possessed.

She lifted his shirt upward, scraped her teeth across his nipple, then tongued it softly. "Take this off before I get impatient and ruin it," she ordered, repeating his command. "This time you're not getting away with leaving anything on."

"Believe me," he assured her. "I want nothing more than to be naked with you, sweetheart." *Naked and tearing down your walls,* he added silently. He kissed her and then set her away from him, immediately tossing his shirt aside.

They stared at each other a moment, stared at the clock, then back at each other. One hour left. One hour would never be enough. In silent agreement, there was a frenzied rush of undressing. Blake made it to his socks and then forgot everything but Darla—standing before him gloriously naked. Her breasts were high, full, with pebble-tight cherry nipples. Her hips were slender, her skin ivory perfection. Every second he was with her, she seemed to grow more beautiful. He stepped toward her.

"Wait," she said, holding up a hand then pointing at this feet. "I said everything off this time."

He didn't argue. He was too hot and too ready for her. He had his socks off in seconds and pulled her into his arms, lifting her. Her legs wrapped around his waist, the wet heat of her core warming his stomach. Lust tore through him, the desire to bury himself inside her and get lost was almost too much to resist.

"Tell me you have a condom," she panted, apparently feeling what he was.

"A half dozen," he said, carrying her to the dresser.

She pulled back and gave him an incredulous look. "Pretty sure of yourself, aren't you?"

"It was one or six. I chose six. But yeah, I'm hoping you'll let me convince you we need all six sometime in the near future." He settled her on top of the dresser and slid his fingers into her hair. "What do I have to do to make that happen?"

She pulled back and stared at him, more of that raw innocence he found so appealing swirling in the depths of her stare. "I don't know... I..."

He leaned in and gently kissed her neck. "We'll talk about that later."

He inched her knees farther apart, skimming his

palms up her thighs, taking in the blond curls and pretty pink flesh, glistening wet with desire.

"You're beautiful," he said, his gaze lifting to hers. "Perfect."

Her cheeks flushed. "Blake," she whispered shyly. He loved that about her. The way she ordered him around one minute, and then turned sweetly vulnerable the next.

It was the vulnerability in her in that moment that got to him, that had him cradling her face and lifting her face to his. "Whatever you're doing to me, keep doing it. I like it."

The way she seemed to have no idea how much she affected him, no intent to use it against him. It only made him want to please her more.

Confusion knitted her brow. "I've pretty much been mad at you the entire time we've known each other."

"Are you mad now?"

"Yes."

"Why?" He caressed her breasts, pressed her backward, her weight on her hands behind her. He licked one pretty pink bud and then the next.

"We never made up," she claimed breathlessly.

"We seem to be getting along pretty well to me," he said, licking her nipple again.

"If you don't get that condom—"

He kissed her. "I don't have to be told twice."

Blake grabbed his jeans, digging out his wallet. He fumbled for the condom. He wanted her so bad he was trembling. That was a first. There were a lot of firsts with Darla. That seemed good. He hoped. He didn't know. He didn't know much of anything right now, except how badly he wanted to be inside her.

She leaned back on the dresser, her breasts thrust high. For a moment, he went still, his throat dry. His cock got impossibly hard. He sheathed himself in seconds as she watched, and then wasted no time returning to her. Wrapping his arm around her slender waist, he slid his fingers in the wet heat of her body to ready her for him. He wanted to be in her, he wanted to feel the wet wonder of her body clenching him tight and holding on. But he wanted this to be good for her. He wanted there to be a reason to use those five other condoms.

"I'm way beyond waiting," she said hoarsely, closing her hand around his shaft and guiding the blunt head of his erection to where she wanted it—telling him she was ready. She was driving him out of his mind with desire. She was hitting all the right marks.

He parted her with his fingers and entered her. She was tight and hot, and he groaned with the pleasure of her muscles contracting around him. An intense urgency built inside him. He thrust deeper inside her and swallowed her gasp with his kiss, a wild, ravenous kiss. Too wild for the dresser—he struggled to fully reach her.

Blake lifted her again and carried her to the mattress. He placed her on the bed beneath him, and she opened for him like a flower—a jasmine-scented flower that he couldn't get enough of. He raised one of her legs over his shoulder and pressed his palm under her perfect ass. He swiveled his hips and drove into her, right where he wanted to be. She had him all now.

He lingered a moment, his eyes searching the depths of hers. He wasn't quite sure what she might see in his eyes, but he couldn't look away. Her fingers traced his lips and he kissed them, then kissed her. He lost himself in the seductive bliss that was her taste, her body. He started to move, to pump into her. What started as slow and cautious quickly became fast and confident. And she met that uncontrollable need—her hands were all over him, her body rocking with his.

He palmed her sweet ass and thrust again and again. Her hips lifted on a moan, her body stiffened. "Blake I…" Her body clenched around him, pulling the pleasure from him, taking it from him. Blake shuddered with his release until his muscles relaxed. He eased her leg down and buried his face in her neck. Long seconds passed and he forced himself to consider time, and work and things he'd rather forget. He had to talk to Darla about why he was here—why they were here—in the first place. He would upset her and he could think of a lot of things that he wanted to do and with the soft and willing female beneath him, and upsetting her wasn't on the list.

11

BLAKE LIFTED UP ON HIS ARMS, his elbows framing Darla's face. "What time is it?" she asked urgently.

He checked the clock. "We have half an hour. We should get dressed." He didn't move.

"Yes," she said, but she didn't move, either. "We should get dressed."

"For the record, I could stay in bed the rest of the day with you and be a happy man."

She reached up and touched his face, her small fingers gentle. The touch sent a rush of renewed heat down his spine. "I'm still mad," she said.

He smiled. He couldn't help himself. He loved the way she dueled with him, the way he knew he had to work to earn her. He loved that she didn't want him just because of who he was or what he could give her.

"In case you missed basic emotion 101," Darla scolded, "anger is not a reason to smile."

"Be angry. Be whatever." His voice sounded gravelly, affected. "Just tell me you don't regret this."

"Blake, I... No. No, I don't." Her tone shifted from a mix of sultry innocence to a stronger one. "Not yet, that is. Not unless you make me late to the set."

Darla scooted to the edge of the bed and he resisted the urge to reach across and shackle her wrist in a gentle hold. He turned to face her, unconcerned about his nakedness. He liked being naked with her. But she wasn't in such a receptive mood. She kept her back to him, as if debating a run for the bathroom.

"Just tell me this," he said, baiting her to turn around, to talk to him. "Why are you so damn feisty, and in my face, but you let Lana run all over you in that audition room?"

She whirled around, her breasts bouncing in a way that he couldn't help but admire. She yanked the sheet up around her, obviously noticing. "Lana isn't running over me."

"Says who?"

"Blake—"

"Meagan noticed. She said you weren't acting like yourself. She's the one who gave me your phone number."

She paled instantly. "What?"

He shook his head. "I was standing at the monitors when you argued with Lana and then walked out of the room for the break. Meagan heard the entire exchange and she commented about you backing down." She ran her hand through her hair, her bottom lip quivering as if she were fighting tears.

He softened his voice. "If this is about us, about Lana's threat—"

"It's not." She swallowed hard. "Not really. I mean, yes, I'm worried about her causing trouble for us, but I'm not sure I'm rational about it, either."

Us. He didn't miss the choice of words, and it pleased him.

Darla continued, "I know I'm not myself and I certainly wasn't myself in that audition room. I hate that Meagan noticed. I hate that I'm letting her down."

"Don't be so hard on yourself. You aren't letting Meagan down." He was both surprised and impressed that she was self-aware enough to know when she wasn't in the right mind-set, that she was open enough with him to say so and to share her fears. "Meagan just wants the real you in that room and on the show. The same you who came storming down the hallway not so long ago, ready to lay into me."

She studied him a long moment, her green eyes glistening with a story he wanted her to tell, but he had a good feeling she wouldn't. Not now, not yet. "Most people in competing time slots wouldn't have told me about this," she finally said. "They'd hope I would fail."

She was right. "I live in this world, Darla. I don't *live* this world." He drew her hand into his. "Talk to me, Darla. Is there something going on with your studio? Did they put some condition on you doing *Stepping Up* that you're struggling with?"

"No." She shook her head, her fingers curling beneath his, telling him he'd hit some sort of nerve. "It's just that…it's complicated." She glanced at the clock. "Oh, God. It's later than I thought. I have to go. We have to go." She dropped the sheet, making a mad dash for the bathroom. Blake tried to catch her, but his damn feet got stuck in the sheet. He had no chance to stop her. No chance to talk to her about the show, about him hosting it or about the next time they could be alone together.

The bathroom door shut with a decisive thud. Blake was shut out. Of everything. She was running from something and he had somehow become a part of that that. Which meant he had to find a way to help her if he wanted a chance with her. And he did. In fact, for a man who hadn't been looking for a woman, he was remarkably ready to do some fighting of his own for that chance—*for her*.

Blake considered his options. Pushing Darla now, when she had to go in front of a camera to face whatever personal demons she was battling wasn't going to earn him points. She wanted space and he had to give it to her. He had to respect what she had ahead of her the rest of the day. He darn sure wasn't throwing her the bombshell that he was going to be around a whole lot more than she thought from outside a bathroom door. No. She wanted him gone now, so he'd be gone. He just wasn't going to like it.

12

DARLA STOOD IN the hotel bathroom with her back against the door and her eyes squeezed shut. She'd run from Blake, run because she was afraid of the emotion he was making her feel. She just had to get away from him before she did something crazy, like fall for him. He felt too right, too good, and her track record—even with him— was proof of the trouble that always followed. And so she stood, naked, with her clothes and her purse on the other side of the door—where he was. Which was where she wanted to be, and knew she had no place being.

She inhaled and, against all reason, willed Blake to knock on the door, to talk her off the ledge. Still, she'd be better off if he didn't and left the room. If he left without a word, in fact, and proved to her that this was about a half dozen condoms and not a half dozen emotions.

Time stretched by and there was no knock. She heard movement, though. He was dressing. Of course, he was dressing. He had to get to the set, just like she did. He'd knock when he was done. He'd say goodbye. He'd ask to see her again and make some sexy remark that referenced using condom number two. That would prove he only wanted sex. That would make this easy. They were supposed to be just about sex. That's why she'd stepped out on this ledge in the first place. It had seemed simple, uncomplicated. An escape she'd desperately needed.

The hotel room door opened and shut. He'd left? She listened, waited. No sound. Nothing. He'd left and had said nothing before doing so. No request for a sex date. No anything. Not even a goodbye. What did that mean? It had to mean he'd read between the lines when she darted away, that he knew she was running scared and he wasn't up for the chase—not that she wanted him to chase her. It wasn't like that. She wasn't sure what she wanted. The knots in her stomach said it wasn't this, though. It wasn't him gone and her in here.

Darla slumped against the bathroom door. She had her answers to the burning questions in her mind, of the possibilities that might exist between her and Blake. This meant there was nothing of substance between them. She should be happy. She wasn't happy.

Darla yanked open the door and raced around the room, gathered her clothing, pulling items on, trying not to think about taking them off while Blake watched. While Blake stood naked in front of her—tall, broad, ripped, gorgeous Blake. She hadn't even had time to fully enjoy just how gorgeous.

She shook away the image and rushed to the door to find her purse where she'd tossed it earlier. She stopped dead in her tracks at the piece of paper sitting on top of it.

Her heart skipped a beat and she barely managed to breathe as she darted for it, a bit too eager. She picked it up and five condoms tumbled to the floor. Her throat went dry. She wasn't sure she wanted to read the note after all.

It wasn't just sex. I figure I can't prove that to you while these puppies are taunting me with the many ways we might use them. And speaking of taunting, don't let Lana win. Show her who is really the boss. Blake

Emotion welled in Darla's chest. She was so falling for this man. She was falling and falling and falling. Hard. She liked him, plain and simple. Too much. Yes— "too much" was a theme for her with Blake. She didn't think it was possible to ignore him, to walk away from this thing between them until she knew where it might lead. *You have to,* a voice in her head said.

Granted, there was more on the line than just her needs and her feelings for Blake. Making this show work wasn't only about her. It was about the parents who'd always been there for her, who'd supported her dreams and her life choices.

She had to go back to the same thing she'd told herself in the bathroom. Her track record with men wasn't one she thought supported a gamble on Blake, not when she owed her parents everything, and they deserved the world.

Darla arrived at a room set up with tables and chairs,

with various wardrobe and toiletries. Allison, who Darla now knew would be her makeup and hair person, was there alone, eating a sandwich. She glanced up at Darla, right as she was about to take a bite, and froze. She set down her food and pushed to her feet. "Finally, you're here! You look like crap."

Darla exhaled. So much for believing she'd doctored her hair and makeup in an acceptable manner. "Well. No one can say you're not honest."

"What the heck did you do on your break?" Allison complained, motioning Darla to a chair. "Sit down— and fast. You're due on set in minutes. The other judges have come and gone."

"Sorry," Darla said, settling into the chair. "I have a case of nerves and lunch didn't sit well. I've been, uh, lying down."

"Oh," Allison said, her brows dipping. "Why are you nervous? You have a show of your own and I love it. Did I mention I'm a fan? Huge, huge fan."

Darla gave her an appreciative smile. "Now you're just saying all the right things, and I prefer the honest, 'you look like crap' kind of communication."

"I said I was a fan. I didn't say you don't look like crap."

Darla laughed. "Okay, then," she conceded. "I stand corrected. Thank you for the compliment and, ah, insult."

"All meant in the most loving of ways," Allison assured her. "I'll fix you all up on one condition."

"Okay," Darla said cautiously, thinking everyone was all about conditions today. "I'll bite. What condition?"

She lowered her voice. "That you put that diva Lana in her place every chance you get this season." She dropped to a whisper. "We're all looking forward to watching it."

Darla absorbed the words, taking them in with surprise. "Who is 'we all'?"

"All the crew," she said, rolling a cart of makeup and hair supplies to Darla's side. "No one likes her. She's just so mean to the contestants. We know you'll stick up for them, like you do for all kinds of people on your show—and the animals. We all love the animal rescue special you do on Fridays."

The comment made her think of her parents, how she had to focus on her agenda to save their ranch. It had suffered from a virus that attacked cattle. Her mother and father hadn't told her how bad it had gotten until it was almost too late and they'd taken on debt they couldn't afford to pay back.

Darla's chest expanded with warmth and understanding as her father's frequently spoken words replayed in her head. Words he'd repeated about their financial struggles. *Honey, things happen for reasons. You have to have faith. Sometimes we just don't know what those reasons are until later.* Darla's fear that Blake was a distraction lifted like a cloud of worry and paranoia. Blake had heard Meagan's concern. Blake had warned her so she could fix what was broken. Blake had made her late enough to the set to have Allison share this piece of information with her. And, most importantly, Blake had

given her good advice. She had to be herself in the audition room or she would disappoint everyone, not just
Meagan. She'd disappoint herself. She'd disappoint her
parents. She had to go into that room and forget about
the pressure, about her parents' predicament. If she did
that, everything would be okay. She had to come through
for them the way they'd always come through for her.

After Allison made up an excuse of burning Darla's
hair with a flat iron to buy more time, Darla managed
to inhale two chocolate bars—Allison agreed chocolate
was safe, even for a sick stomach—and she was ready
for work. She was ready for Lana. She wasn't, however,
ready to see Blake. Or to say goodbye. But she had to.

THE AUDITIONS HAD BEEN TAKING place for a good three
hours when Blake wished a young male dancer good
luck in Vegas, and then found himself being flagged
down by Meagan. She lifted her hand and motioned for
him to follow her.

Blake froze in an "uh-oh" moment. He'd been hoping
for a break to check on Meagan and hoping, even more
so, to find out if she'd shaken off her morning. He now
prayed he wasn't about to find out the opposite, a fear
easily conceived considering Meagan had made her sus-
picions about him and Darla obvious. She'd also made it
clear she suspected that Blake was negatively influenc-
ing Darla. Hell, Darla thought he was, too—or at least,
that was what he'd now surmised about the bathroom
incident. And maybe he was. Maybe he needed to keep
his distance, no matter how much he wanted to have

Darla up close and personal. Not forever, but for now, until she found her footing on the show.

Blake followed Meagan to an empty event room that had been cleared as a contestant holding room. "What did you say to Darla at break?" she asked immediately, going right for the gut.

Blake felt the blow, and while he wasn't one to be at a loss for words, it took him a minute to recover. "Not anything different than I imagine you would have," he replied cautiously.

She studied him, as she had earlier and then waved off his words. "Details aren't important. Whatever you said, it worked and that's all that counts. She's back to her normal self in there and I couldn't be happier. Now, I feel free to actually talk to both of you about an idea my team has been bouncing around since early this morning when we found out about Rick."

"Talk to us?" he asked, a warning alarm going off in his head.

"Meagan," Darla said, appearing in the doorway and going white as a sheet as soon as she spotted Blake. She was as worried as he was that this was about them.

"You needed me?" she asked Meagan.

"Come in," Meagan encouraged. "And pull the door shut."

"I'll get it," Blake offered quickly. He closed the door and stepped in between the two women so he could gauge both of their facial expressions as this—whatever it was—went down. "Since Rick isn't coming back—" Meagan started.

"Rick isn't coming back?" Darla asked, her tone rippling with shock.

Meagan's gaze flicked Blake a "you didn't tell her?" look, before she replied, "No. He's not. He'll be recuperating for a while. As you know, Blake is filling in for Rick today, but I've thrown his name in the ring for a potential long-term replacement."

Darla gaped, her attention jerking to Blake's with accusation. "You're taking over for Rick?"

Could he get any more sideswiped? "I'm just rolling with the punches," he assured her, darting Meagan a warning glance. "I've agreed to nothing but helping out today. Maybe a few audition shows forward, if needed. Beyond that, nothing is even somewhat final."

"About your future with the show," Meagan said. "I just hung up from a conference call with your agent—who wants you to call him—and one of the studio executives." She glanced at Darla. "Right after I had a conversation with your agent and one of your studio executives."

Blake's spine stiffened and he could feel the tension emanating from Darla. He could almost hear her suck in a breath at the same time he did, waiting for what was about to come next, no doubt, thinking what he was thinking.

Was one or both of them about to be fired?

13

"I DON'T UNDERSTAND," BLAKE heard Darla say in a strained voice, her ivory skin pasty white. "Is there some sort of a problem with me being on the show because Blake is now potentially the host?"

"Because if there is," Blake said sternly, praying that he hadn't misjudged the situation. "Count me out of the show. I'll head home and stay there."

Meagan looked between the two of them, a keen expression on her face. "You'd walk away from a huge paycheck because it puts Darla in jeopardy?"

"Yes," he said at the same time Darla said, "No."

"No, you will not," Darla added, frowning at Blake. "This is your studio, not mine. You belong here."

"You both belong here," Meagan interrupted.

"I'm perfectly happy doing just my show." Blake focused on Darla. "The big Hollywood scene has never been my thing. *Stepping Up* works for me, not because of the big prime-time format, but because of the fans and the contestants. Those things hit the same hot buttons as my show."

"This is money and opportunity, as well," Darla said, being humble and generous, as he'd expect of her. But when she curled her fingers inside her palms, he could see she was shaking. She wanted this. She wanted it bad, and still she added fiercely, "You can't walk away from this."

"I'm not invested in this like you are," he reasoned. "I *can* walk away. And I will, if it has to be one or the other, you or me. It's the right thing to do."

"It's not," Meagan said firmly, drawing their attention. "This *is* a great opportunity. You're right about that, Darla. A great opportunity for *both* of you."

"What?" Darla asked. "I thought…so, wait. There's not a problem with Blake and I working together?"

"I never said there was," Meagan informed her. "You two just took a piece of what I was saying and ran with it. Nobody has a problem with the two of you working together. At least, not now that they've heard my plan. In fact, they're thrilled with the plan I've suggested. It's the two of you that I have to convince now."

Darla cast Blake a cautious look. "So," she said contemplatively, "let me just be sure I understand. My show being on a competing network, in a competing time slot with Blake, isn't an issue?"

"It's a bonus," Meagan asserted, "and the key to my team's plan to boost ratings this season."

"What are we missing here, Meagan?" Blake asked skeptically.

"Everyone at the bar last night noticed the combative chemistry the two of you have and they found it entertaining. Add to it the past history with the shoe incident, and people are interested to see how you might clash, or not clash, again."

"Oh, wow," Darla murmured. "Were we that obvious last night?"

"You say that like it's a problem," Meagan chided. "It's not. In fact, it's the opposite. It's magical, and a way to make this season unique. That's what we need— a way to keep the show from becoming repetitive and boring. Last season we had the curse. This season, two competing television personalities."

"Are we talking about some sort of format change for the show or a role change for myself or Darla?" Blake asked. "Because as it is, Darla and I won't be interacting much."

"The judges and the host have plenty of interaction during the live shows," she corrected. "Which is what we want to play up."

"Play up?" Darla asked. "I'm not following, Megan."

"The details will have to be fine-tuned based on your input. But what we know for certain is that we'll emphasize a rivalry between you two and tease the audience with the battle and/or sparks that might fly."

Blake's brow lifted. "Sparks?" His gaze flickered to Darla, who had turned paler still when he hadn't thought she could do so.

"Viewers love a good rivalry," Meagan explained. "They will either want you to clash or want you to fall into each other's arms. It will be a fun battle of the sexes theme we can use."

"I know you mean it when you say this is going to be good for the show and for us," Darla said. "And I believe you when you say that the studio is supportive of this idea, but I'm concerned this could backfire on me. I'm looking for longevity, not my fifteen minutes of fame. I'm the outsider, the one from a competing network. One misstep that makes them see me as having allegiances to this network over them could cost me my job."

"*One* of your jobs," Meagan said. "But you aren't going to leave either show on anyone's terms but your own. You're too good to have this end any differently."

"You don't know that," Darla argued. "This first season for me is more like an audition," she glanced at Blake, "and we all know it. If I get bad feedback from the audience, I'm gone."

"You won't," Blake said, unwilling to let her allow fear to affect her decision-making. He might not be a hot Hollywood star, but he knew opportunity when he saw it. "They'll love you just like your audience loves you."

"This is a different format from my show," Darla said. "I'll be openly critiquing people's performances, building and destroying dreams. Blake won't have that pressure, nor will he have the competing network issue."

"*Stepping Up* is going to be highly invested in you both," Meagan assured her. "We'll be doing a print and television campaign featuring the two of you. Any way you look at that, you two are the reasons both networks get this exposure—and Darla, your network gets it for free. *Because of you.* It's a sweet deal for them. Call your agent and your producer and talk it out at the next break."

"She's right, Darla," Blake said. "It's a sweet deal for your network—and even mine, for that matter. They win ratings and advertisers."

Darla shook her head, rejecting his encouragement. "Ultimately we're still competitors, Blake. The last one standing keeps their show and this one right along with it. You know that's how this ends."

"I don't know any such thing," Blake said. "And you could easily have this network pay you enough to make your show a nonissue."

She narrowed her gaze. "And you get rid of me as a competitor?"

"No," he objected. "Come on, Darla. You know better than that."

"How?" she asked. "How do I know better? I barely know you. And we both know our new variety-type shows could stay on the air for twenty years. Prime time rarely hits five seasons. Keeping our day jobs makes sense."

"Hey," Meagan sniped, "don't be numbering our days already. We are going to keep this show new and fresh, just like we're trying to do with you two injected into the season full-throttle now.

"Your daytime shows are your daytime shows," Megan assured her. "The idea is simply that this show gets your shows more exposure." She glanced at her watch. "Yikes! Okay. We don't have much time. You both have concerns. I understand fully, but I sincerely think you will be glad you did this. So let me just arm you both with information to think about and to talk to your representation about." She glanced at Blake. "Blake, we don't need you at every audition since we don't shoot those segments live. We piece together random footage for audition segments. This gives us time to finish planned shows in New York and pretape others to give you breathing room. Vegas week is when we select the final twelve dancers, which will be crazy insanity, with emotions high and contestants sleep-deprived. But it's also a perfect time to do some playful rival clash stuff between the two of you. We'll talk through details. I have ideas. Lots of ideas." She let out a breath. "That brings me to the here and now. Blake, the studio wants to see you at eight tomorrow morning to talk about contract terms and how you are going to juggle two shows. That means you need to go catch a flight to NY now. Your agent is working on finding you one."

"What?" Blake asked, taken off guard. "That's fast, Meagan." The idea of leaving without the opportunity to talk to Darla was really *not* a good one. "Surely, the studio can wait until later tomorrow."

Meagan shook her head. "Darla is here to stay no matter what. She's contracted. But if we can't work this out with you, Blake, I have to find a new host. I need to know where we are headed. If you manage to nail down a contract, and Darla and her agent agree to everything as well, then Darla and I will fly back to New York to meet with everyone involved right after the next audition. We'll shoot promos and ad campaigns then."

A knock sounded on the door and Jimmy rushed inside, not waiting on an answer. "We need you and Darla back on set. And Blake, your agent called. You need to leave for the airport about fifteen minutes ago. I have a car waiting."

Damn it, Blake cursed silently.

"We're coming," Meagan called to Jimmy, then lowered her voice. "I'm thrilled about this. The possibilities the two of you represent for this season are endless."

Jimmy shouted again and Meagan nodded to Darla. "We better go." She started walking, and Darla cast Blake one long, meaningful look before she fell into step behind Meagan. She was creating reasons to make him the enemy. Blake stared after her, fighting the urge to grab her and pull her aside. Better yet, to grab her and kiss her, and remind her of what they'd shared. But then, like in the airplane, he held back. He was going to have to leave and wait to talk to Darla when he landed. That is, if she would take his calls.

DARLA FINALLY ENTERED her hotel room at eleven o'clock that evening after a very emotional day. She locked the door behind her and then froze instantly as her nostrils flared with a familiar scent. Blake's scent. She wasn't sure if she wanted to thank housekeeping for apparently not doing their job, or complain to management, considering the vivid images the smell provoked—delicious, naughty, wonderful images of her and Blake together. Images that were more proof of how conflicted she was over the man. It made her feel like she'd been naive, like he was using her. And yet, another image of the two of them against the wall, his hands on her breasts, his body pressed to hers, had her shoving away from the door and shaking her head. She was so very conflicted. Darla tossed her purse on the bed and dropped like a rock beside it onto her back, her legs dangling off the mattress. She had to be up early in the morning to fly to New Mexico with Meagan for the next round of auditions. They were going to talk more about the show then as well, and about Blake, although there wasn't much left to discuss at this point. Darla had spent a few short minutes on the phone with her agent, who had made it clear that not only did her contract allow for everything proposed, he had no idea why she wouldn't want to do it in the first place. This was exposure, money, all the perks. Her producer had been thrilled, as well. High ratings meant job stability for everyone involved in her daytime show. Neither her agent nor her producer seemed concerned about the things that concerned her, like the possibility that a short-term gain could lead to a crashing and burning. Everyone was so focused on the ratings now, now, now, that they weren't seeing the future. And money. It was always about money. It had never been that to her, but maybe that was wrong. Money allowed her to care for people she loved. To snub her nose at it would be crazy.

"The future, *your future,* could be *Stepping Up,*" she said to the empty room.

One door closes and another opens, her father's voice in her head added. The man had too many sayings and made too much sense. She wanted to call him, to tell him what she was feeling, to ask his advice. He'd make her feel better, but at what price? This time, it was her place to make him feel better. It was her role to make sure he knew everything was going to be okay.

Darla realized her phone was vibrating, still on silent from when she'd been filming. Shoot. It was probably her parents. She had to shake off her mood and be cheerful. She was going to have to resist the urge to do what she always did, and tell them everything.

Darla grabbed her purse and dug out her phone only to see a text come through. It's Blake was all the message read.

Darla stared at the text, waiting for him to say something more, but he didn't. She told herself not to respond, but the truth was, she was going to see him and see him plenty. Hiding from him wasn't an answer. Running from him wouldn't get her far. No. Blake was in her life to stay. Proof yet again that she was not only lousy at choosing her dates, she was lousy at choosing one-night stands.

She punched the pad of her phone and typed, It's Darla.

His reply was instant. The same Darla who won't answer her phone?

She punched the history on her phone and realized she'd missed four calls—all in the past hour. Her parents had called once. Blake owned the other three attempts.

Darla considered the situation, then typed I don't like to talk on the phone.

You're mean to me was his reply.

You're very perceptive, she typed back before she could stop herself.

I guess you don't want to know what I'm going to say in the meeting tomorrow, then.

She sat up and stared at the phone, then punched the call button. The instant he answered, she said, "That was manipulation, just like when you called me and told me to meet you by my room."

"Guilty," he agreed. "But both times were with good intentions."

"You knew about this hosting thing and didn't tell me," she accused, shifting the conversation to the thing that had bothered her all day long.

"Not guilty on that one," he said. "I—"

"*You didn't* tell me."

"I would have," he argued, "but once again you tucked tail and ran from me." She opened her mouth to deny it and he added, "And don't tell me you didn't, because we both know you did. That left me with two options. Tell you about the possible hosting job through the bathroom door so you had something to worry about besides Lana, or wait to tell you this evening, when you had put Lana behind you. I chose the latter and knowing what a worrier you are, I'd do it again. Unfortunately, Meagan's time line to deal with Rick's departure bit me in the ass. And speaking of being bitten in the proverbial ass, what was that about me trying to smash your show? That was a low blow."

Darla cringed inwardly. "You hadn't told me about the hosting thing."

"And that makes me a low-down dirty snake?"

"No."

"And?"

And what? "Okay. I tend to just react rather than think first when I feel trapped. I need to work on that. I'm sorry."

"Do you believe I want to destroy your show?"

"Before this conversation or after?"

"So you believed it when you said it?"

"I already admitted I reacted to being cornered," she admitted, and reluctantly added, because he deserved to have it said, "I know that you could have thrown me under the Lana bus, and you didn't."

He was silent a moment. "Did you talk to your agent?"

"Yes. You?"

"Yes."

"And?" she prodded.

"You first."

"Fine. He said a few good years on a prime-time show could equal more money and opportunity than twenty years on my daytime show."

"Why do I sense a *but?*"

"I just don't like the instability of being camera talent," she confessed, surprised at how easily she shared her feelings with him. "I liked casting because I knew I had a job—a stable job I could count on. This is like gambling all the time on the right step for this level of career or that level of career."

"I felt that same thing when I started out," he admitted. "But I invested well as soon as I had the money to do so, and I made sure I was secure even if I lose the show."

"Investing has never been my thing." But it was smart. She knew it was.

"Maybe you should watch my show," he teased, and then added, "And warning. If my father comes to any of these tapings, and he finds out you don't invest, he'll insist on it."

If his father came to any of the shows. "So. I guess that means you're taking the job?"

"My agent wants me to. We'll see how it goes with the studio. You really don't want me to take it, do you?"

No. Yes. She wanted him. That seemed a potential problem. "I'm conflicted."

"About me doing the show or about Meagan's plan or—"

"About all of it, but you in particular."

"I see," he drawled. "Well. Why don't we work on that when you come back to New York two days from now?" His voice was low, sensual.

Her body instantly reacted, heating up. His scent everpresent. "I'll only go back to New York if you take the job."

"That sounds like an incentive to me."

The way he said the words rushed over her and panic set in. She was going to wind up caring for this man, and either get hurt or ruin her career. "We can't see each other on a personal level. Not when we have to work so closely together. Had I known any of this was going to happen, I would never have started this."

More thick silence filled the air. "Okay," he agreed finally.

Okay? "Okay?" Her voice quivered and so did the muscles in her stomach. She didn't know why. She did know why. She didn't want to admit why.

"Isn't that what you wanted me to say?"

No, but it was the right answer, even if she didn't want it to be. "Yes."

"Fine then. I'll let you go. We both have big days tomorrow."

She inhaled. "Okay." She really hated that word.

"Good night, Darla," he said softly, and hung up.

She stared at the phone, emotion welling in her chest. And she didn't know how it happened, but she punched redial. "That's it?" she demanded when he answered. "Good night?" He laughed. "Don't laugh, Blake." He laughed again and she repeated, "I said—"

"Don't laugh. I know. I already told you that I'm crazy about you, Darla. That hasn't changed. But I've yet to hear you make one statement that says you feel the same about me. I'm no glutton for punishment. You want this to be all business, we'll make it all business."

She didn't know what to say. She liked him. She wanted him. She was just so damn…conflicted. "Okay." She hung up before she defined what she was saying *okay* to. Hung up! She pressed her hand to her face. Could she make more of a fool of herself with this man?

14

BLAKE HAD TAKEN THE HOSTING job. Now, three days after hanging up on her new coworker rival former lover, Darla was back in New York and about to see him for the first time since then. With a garment bag thrown over her shoulder, she stood outside the twentieth-floor studio of renowned photographer to the stars, Frankie Masse. He was shooting the promos for *Stepping Up*.

She reached for the door but pulled back, nervous not because Frankie had been an intimidating and bossy man during her solo shoot at his studio the day before, but because of Blake. Yes. She was, without question, ridiculously nervous about seeing Blake again.

"Is the door locked?"

Darla jumped at the unexpected sound of his voice. "Blake." Her hand balled on her chest at his presence, suddenly finding him so close she could reach up and touch him. And she wanted to. "I didn't hear the elevator. You scared me."

His blue eyes swept over the ivory suit that Frankie

had requested her to wear. He wore a black suit himself, the dark color a dramatic contrast to her lighter one. The expression on his face was both intimate and familiar, perhaps mimicking her own. He was remembering— just as she was, she had no doubt—how intimate and familiar they'd been together. She had been thinking a lot about Blake, and not just about the pleasure-filled moments in that hotel room. But also about their banter on the plane and the way he'd come to her rescue with Lana. The way his eyes danced with mischief at times when someone else's would burn with anger.

"You must have had something pretty intense on your mind," he suggested, his voice a gentle caress—a *knowing* caress. "Because the elevator creaks like an old man with arthritis."

"I guess I did," she admitted, realizing exactly what was bothering her and what she had to do. "About the phone call the other night—"

"When you hung up on me?"

Her lips thinned. "You hung up on me first."

"I said, 'Good night.' You just said 'Okay.'"

"Because *you* said, 'Okay.'"

His eyes narrowed. "Isn't that what you wanted me to say?"

She wet her lips, his eyes following the movement. Heat pooled low in her belly. No. No, it wasn't what she'd wanted him to say and that was the problem. Or maybe it wasn't really a problem. Maybe she was needlessly making it a problem. She wanted to just say that to him, to talk to him. That brought her clarity. She trusted

Blake enough to tell him how vulnerable she felt and that meant something. It meant he was worth taking a risk on.

She drew in a breath and let it out. "What I wanted, or rather, what I want—" she started to say, but the elevator creaked open as loudly as he had claimed.

"Is the door locked?" Meagan said from behind Blake.

"Saved by the proverbial bell," Blake said softly, before stepping to the side to greet Meagan. "We just arrived. We were about to go inside."

"Excellent, then," Meagan replied, waving them forward. "Let's get snapping those photos. I'd like to actually give myself and Darla a chance to relax before we head to Chicago at the crack of dawn tomorrow morning."

"Of course," Blake said, expecting Darla to step away from him. Instead, she leaned in, looking him in the eyes.

"You keep assuming I need, or want, to be saved." She threw open the door to the photography room, just as she had opened the door to the possibilities between herself and Blake.

TIME TICKED BY SLOWLY WHILE Blake waited on Darla to be out of hair and makeup for the photo shoot. He was thinking about their exchange in the hallway. Thinking about how much he wanted it to be enough. Enough to take her home with him tonight. Enough to hold her again—if not now, sometime soon. Enough to take the risk to get to know her better.

He shifted from foot to foot and leaned against the

wall framing a massive window overlooking the city. He'd seen the heat in Darla's stare, the desire glinting in the depths of her beautiful green eyes. Desire. Lust. An attraction that they seemed to generate when they were anywhere near each other. But he'd also seen her hesitation to answer his question about their phone call. She didn't need saving. She wasn't any more certain about him than she had been before. And the thing was, he was on uncertain ground of his own. Blake had never felt this way about a woman and he didn't know if that made it important that he press her now, or just the opposite. Maybe he needed to back off, to let her run. A few of his father's words echoed in his mind. *Son. You never want anything that doesn't come honest.*

Blake scrubbed his jaw. Damn it. He didn't want anything that wasn't honest from Darla—anything not genuine. He couldn't push Darla. He *wouldn't* push her. It had to come honest. *They* had to come honest.

"Let's get started," Frankie shouted. "Blake and Darla, I need you in the center of the room."

Blake shoved off the wall to find three of Frankie's staff members gathering nearby, while Meagan stepped away to take a call on her cell. Frankie waved Blake to a twelve-by-twelve squared-off area floored with white tiles and enclosed by hardwood, umbrellas and cameras. Darla appeared at the opposite edge of the set.

Her gaze swept over him and came to rest on his face. She actually managed to scald him with a look of pure lust in the same instant that she damned him for apparently making her do so. Would she ever figure out her feelings for him?

"Okay, Blake and Darla," Meagan said, shoving her slim phone back into snug, faded jeans. "One of the studio bigwigs is in town, and he and several of the show's top sponsors want to meet us all for dinner." She eyed her watch. "They made reservations for seven, which is going to make it tight for me to get home and change. If either of you have a reason to get us out of this that they'll buy, speak up now, please."

"Ten years in this business has taught me to say 'yes' as often as possible," Blake commented. "There will be more important times when you'll have to say 'no.'"

"Considering I'm with a competing network," Darla said, "I don't think it would get me brownie points to miss this."

"You work for both networks," Meagan corrected. "I wish you'd start feeling like you belong here." She grinned. "Blake, I really don't like how right you are, but okay. Dinner it is." She cast Darla a wistful look. "We'll have time to sleep on the plane."

"Have you flown with Darla?" Blake asked, disbelievingly. "Because she won't be sleeping—and neither will you if you're sitting next to her."

"Right," Meagan said drily. "Yes, I have, and you make another good point. Sorry, Darla. I might need to get my seat changed."

Darla sighed. "I understand. Send a new victim, I mean passenger, my way. I'll torture them so you can sleep."

Blake and Meagan started laughing, but so did Darla, just as she had in the hallway when she'd tripped, even in front of Lana. He liked her lack of airs, her willingness to be herself and to not take herself so seriously.

"Are we ready to get this moving?" Frankie asked testily.

Meagan stepped out of the way. "They're all yours."

"Both of you cross your arms in front of your chests," Frankie ordered immediately, "and stare each other down in challenge."

"That shouldn't be a problem for us," Blake said, refocusing on Darla and doing as Frankie directed.

"Not a problem at all," Darla agreed, mimicking his stance by folding her arms in front of her chest, her slim jacket defining her petite waist and flaring out to accent her womanly curves.

Frankie started snapping photos. "Good," he shouted, showing more excitement than Blake thought the man had in him. "Good. Darla. Step closer to Blake."

Darla didn't move. Blake arched a brow. "Thought you didn't need to be saved?"

A look of surprise flashed on her face, as if her hesitation had been instinctive and she hadn't realized what she'd done. She stepped forward. "I don't. In fact, I'd venture to say that if anyone needs to be saved, it's you."

"Love the anger, Darla!" Frankie shouted, as if she intended her attitude for the camera.

"Anger?" Darla repeated, still looking at Blake.

"You do sound pretty angry."

"I'm not angry," she insisted. "I'm not. I'm—"

"Conflicted," Blake supplied.

"Not anymore," she corrected.

"You seem conflicted to me."

"I'm not."

"Closer to each other," Frankie yelled. "I want you almost toe-to-toe, and Darla, give him another prickly stare."

"Prickly," Darla repeated, turning toward the camera. "I was not prickly and I'm not angry."

"Look at Blake!" Frankie ordered.

Darla jerked her gaze back to Blake, looking like a scolded child. He laughed. She glared.

"That's the anger I want," Frankie approved. "Closer, though. Closer."

"You laugh at the most inappropriate times," Darla scolded. She inched forward, leaving no room for Frankie to complain now that the tips of her high heel shoes were touching the tips of Blake's shoes.

He could smell her perfume, floral and soft. "Says who?"

"I imagine everyone who's experienced it."

"Is that right?"

"It is. Maybe that's your way of hiding from whatever it is that's being said."

"Hiding?" he said. "You're accusing *me* of hiding?"

"That's right. Hiding."

"Back to back," Frankie directed. "Backs touching, arms folded in front of your bodies again."

Darla turned. Blake laughed and rotated, then stepped backward, bringing them into direct contact. The connection delivered a jolt of awareness he'd foolishly been unprepared for. Heat sizzled a path through every nerve ending he had.

"Still laughing?" she challenged with a soft taunt for his ears only. She was feeling it, too—the sizzle. The heat.

Blake lowered his voice, ready to taunt in reply. "I didn't run into the bathroom and lock the door." He expected a quick jab back. He didn't get it.

There was a moment of silence, a thickening of the air, before she said, all signs of taunting gone, "I regret doing that. I regret it a lot."

The emotion he heard in her confession and radiating from her body language caught him off guard. "Don't," he started. "Do—"

"Lean back farther. Both of you," Frankie interrupted, and the instant they complied, a slew of pictures followed. Another pose, then another. Frankie kept the camera snapping until he sent them to opposite sides of the set to allow his crew to set up props.

A minute or two later, Blake was sitting in an office chair, while she sat on top of a desk, her legs crossed. Her long, gorgeous legs, he noted. "Roll the chair closer to Darla," Frankie directed Blake. "Darla, I want you to spike that high heel into his chest."

"No!" Meagan said, laughing. "They have a history with shoes and I've already lost one host to an injury."

"I'll be gentle," Darla promised, grinning at Meagan before fixing Blake with a mischievous look. "Though, it's awfully tempting to give him a little roughing up."

"Hurts so good," Blake assured her, motioning to her foot. "Bring it on." He rolled a little closer to her.

"Wait." Frankie motioned to several crew members, before giving Blake and Darla his back to huddle with the others. Blake seriously doubted that they were talking about a camera lens, but he knew an opportunity when he saw it.

Blake rolled the chair around so that only Darla could see his face. "About the bathroom—" he started.

"I ran," she finished for him quietly, glancing toward the others to make sure they still weren't paying them any mind. "I started freaking out about my job and—"

"And that's okay," he said, meaning it. He could barely contain the urge to touch her, but he was all too experienced with the camera to know it too easily captured what you didn't want captured. "It was an honest reaction to an honest emotion." Their eyes locked and held for several silent moments. "Honest is what I'm looking for. And I promise you, no matter how much this business defies you believing it, you won't get anything less from me."

Surprise lit her expression, her eyes softened from bright to light green. "I believe you."

Blake felt the warmth of her growing confidence. He'd never wanted a woman like he did this one, and it was all he could do to remind himself that this was a tiny step forward, not more. Not enough. Not yet.

"Let's go," Frankie said. "Darla. Spike that heel onto his chest. Gently, please. Save the rough stuff for later."

Darla's tongue darted over her red lips. "Later it is." She pressed her heel to his chest.

Instinctively, Blake's hand went to her calf.

Darla shivered, and he was pretty sure he shook on the inside. And only from a small, simple touch. Darla's claim of "it's complicated" came to his mind and he amended his thoughts. There was nothing simple about what this woman did to him.

"No touching!" Frankie ordered. "You aren't supposed to like each other."

"We don't," Darla assured Frankie, staring intently into Blake's eyes.

Blake took his hand away. "Not at all," he agreed.

Blake had promised himself when he'd ended that phone call with Darla back in Denver that he would take things slow with her from here on out, that he would backtrack and make up for rushing too fast out of the gate and into bed. But as he sat there, her skirt riding high on her toned thighs, her delicate knees opened just wide enough to tease him, his cock mercilessly stretched against his zipper and he knew he was in for a rough ride. Oh, yeah. He was definitely in for the rough stuff later, when he might be the one to walk away from a chance to use those five condoms. Because he would, because he had to, if he wanted more than sex with Darla. And he did, he realized with certainty. He did.

Tonight would be a test of his willpower, which he'd always considered solid. Until Darla.

15

EVEN THREE HOURS AFTER the sexually charged photo session, Blake's body still hummed with awareness, with desire, for Darla. It didn't seem to matter that she sat across but several seats down from him at the rectangular table of the happening uptown Italian eatery. She was nowhere near close enough for him to accidentally touch her or to draw in that delicate floral scent of hers.

"Excuse me," the stuffed studio shirt he'd been talking ratings with said when his phone rang. "I've been expecting this call." The man pushed to his feet and headed in search of privacy.

For the millionth time since arriving at the restaurant, Blake's gaze gravitated toward Darla, where she chatted stiffly with Mark Mercer, another studio exec whom Blake both knew and disliked. Mark was also enjoying Darla's time far too much for comfort. Blake wasn't sure who he was more irritated with, though. Mark, for managing to sit next to Darla. Or Darla, for clearly enjoying his company.

"Well, thank you, gentlemen, but it's time for me to head back to the hotel." Meagan rose to her feet as various members of the group followed. Finally, this little piece of hell was over, Blake thought, as he stood up with the rest of their party.

"Can I share a taxi with you?" Mark asked Darla. "I think we're going in the same direction." His tone was friendly and casual, but the look in his eyes was the opposite. Blake found himself sucking in a quiet breath and holding it, waiting for Darla's reply. Darla would say no. He knew she would say no. *If,* he added silently, he hadn't misjudged her ambition.

"Sorry to have to decline," Darla replied, sounding as if she meant it in a tight, forced kind of way. "I actually have a friend from out of town meeting me here for drinks in a few minutes."

Air escaped from Blake's lips and his muscles relaxed, telling him just how important her response had really been to him. Only then did he allow himself to admit the truth. In the back of his mind, worry had been alive and well. Worry that Darla's need to please everyone associated with *Stepping Up* would spell trouble.

Blake curled his fingers into his palms as he watched Mark slide his hand around her waist and whisper something in her ear. Darla gave a forced laugh in response before the man turned away from her. Darla's gaze found Blake's, and he felt the impact immediately. She affected him so easily—too easily. For just an instant, he wasn't overly comfortable with that. But then her expression softened and he could feel her reaching out to him. She wasn't meeting anyone. Neither was she leaving with the group. She didn't want him to, either. And though he knew he should, knew that distance would provide the willpower he needed to slow things down between them, there wasn't a chance in hell that he wasn't leaving here without her. He also wasn't about to make that obvious.

Blake wished her a casual good-night and followed the group to the front of the restaurant. Like the gentleman his parents raised, he hit the corner to flag the needed cabs, starting with one for Meagan.

She stepped forward, but stopped at the cab door to say, "There's still something going on with Darla." It was a warning rather than a question. "You two have chemistry. I like you together. But if the public figures out you're together, like I have, then the advertising tease we're doing—the daytime enemies come together in prime time—it won't work. The tease will be gone. Stay low-key. Don't let this affect the show. You know how studios are. On top one day and kicked to the curb the next. There are too many jobs on the line, too many lives changed, to blow this."

"We'll be careful," Blake promised. "You have my word."

She studied him for a moment longer and started to slide into the car. "Meagan." She paused in midmotion, giving him a questioning look. "I appreciate the way you shoot straight," he said. "It's a rare quality in this business. With you, I'll do the same."

She smiled warmly. "You better."

ONCE BLAKE WAS THE ONLY ONE left standing on the sidewalk, he could feel the charge of anticipation of what was to come—of him and Darla being alone, even if it was in a public place.

He turned to go back inside the restaurant, only to find Darla standing behind him, her garment bag swung over her shoulder. Somehow she appeared a few inches shorter than he remembered. His gaze dropped to her feet, where her heels had been replaced with flats.

She glanced down and then back up. "A girl learns practicality when she lives in this city. My apartment's only a few blocks from here. I'm going to walk it."

"What about your friend that's meeting you?"

Her lips lifted slightly. That amazing awareness between them was back, and he wondered if the people milling on the sidewalk were feeling the charge. "His name is Blake," she finally said. "So glad you made it." Her voice was a caress, a promise.

He knew this could be a big mistake, but still, he found himself smiling and moving toward her. "I'll walk with you. What do you have in that bag, anyway?"

"Frankie had me bring three changes of clothes in case he hated one or more of my options, which he was sure he would," she said, handing him the bag. "He's a very cranky man."

"Artistic types that are too talented for their own good can be that way," he said.

"Very true," she agreed. She pointed to her right. "I'm this way." She wet her lips. Damn, every time she did that his body reacted. He really was ridiculously, insanely, affected by this woman.

He nodded, and they started walking. "What time do you fly out in the morning?" he asked, trying to get his mind back on the present and not on the bedroom that could be in their future.

"Eight. Which means leaving my apartment by six."

"Ouch. That stings."

"I'm not complaining," she said. "I feel blessed to have this opportunity. It's just a little challenging to film my morning show in between auditions. It'll be easier once I'm filming from the L.A. studios. And now that I put Lana in her place, I'm enjoying the auditions. I don't want to worry that I'm going to deliver poor quality content and disappoint my audience."

"I'm glad to hear you feel things are settled down with Lana, and you have a loyal audience so I don't think you have to worry. They watch because of your reactions to situations and your personality, not because of the setting you're in." He cast her a sideways glance and watched as a slight breeze dusted blond wisps of her hair across her pale cheek. Everything male inside him stirred, but there was more. There was emotion—unfamiliar and potent. Emotion that drove him to the burning questions that demanded to be answered. "You've conquered the Lana problem. What about flying? Are you handling that any better than you did that studio guy hitting on you tonight?"

She stopped and turned to him, her eyes flashing with rebuttal. "I handled him just fine."

"So you admit he was hitting on you?"

"I know what he was doing."

"You could have shut down his nonsense but you didn't."

"I was polite and standoffish. It's what girls do in that type of situation."

Right. "I guess."

"You guess? What did you want me to do? Make a fool of him so he hates me? Make everyone think he's an idiot? And because I'm reading an underlying meaning here, it had nothing to do with his position at the studio. I would never blatantly make someone feel bad."

"He was using your eagerness to please the studio to corner you."

"He's a jerk," she agreed. "But that doesn't mean I have to be. I was brought up better and smarter than that. It's a small industry, one that breeds enemies without having to look for them."

Damn. "You're right," he said, suddenly relaxing. He hadn't even realized until that moment just how tense he'd felt. "I'm sorry. I just get irritated at the entire casting couch mentality in this business. I wanted to belt him one."

Her expression softened. "I appreciate that, but I'm a big girl. I can handle myself. I tried to do exactly as you suggested earlier. Choose my battles smartly."

He shook his head. "I'm sorry. I shouldn't have put you on the defensive like that."

"Then why did you?" she asked, narrowing her gaze at him.

He didn't offer some fancy talking-in-circles reply. He wanted honesty; he had to give honesty. "I just want to know who you are, Darla. I want to know the real you. Not the public persona."

"There's no difference for me, Blake," she declared without so much as a blink of an eye. "I am all I know how to be."

An old, suppressed memory surfaced, and with it more raw emotions. A memory of a time when he had been young and naive, riding a wave of early success.

"Who burned you, Blake?" Darla asked softly, drawing his gaze, which had drifted to the pavement.

The question stopped him cold. How easily she had read him, read what he was denying even to himself. A name ran through his mind, a name he hadn't allowed himself to say, even silently, in years.

He shoved away the memory. He wasn't ready to talk about this. Hell, he hadn't even wanted to *think* about it. He hadn't even realized just how easily *he could* think about it. It—*she*—happened ten flipping years ago. He hadn't really loved her. He'd…

Suddenly, Darla held his hand. "Tell me when you're ready." She motioned them forward. "Let's walk."

He wasn't sure she could have done anything more perfect in that moment, giving him a pass but also giving him an open door, not to mention her understanding.

A few seconds passed and he gave a quick nod. They started walking again, both staring up at the dark sky, dotted with stars. And with each step, he felt himself relax. It was a comfortable night, no longer humid and not yet cold and all the more enjoyable because of Darla.

"Are you keeping your morning show focused on *Stepping Up* throughout the auditions?"

"Only a short segment for each show," she said. "I'm afraid to overdo it and drive away viewers who crave the usual things on the show. What about you?" She pointed and they turned down a tree-lined street with rows of condolike housing.

"I'm going to incorporate the travel destinations as much as I can. For instance, my dad's coming to Vegas Week. We're doing a mechanical-bull-riding competition with a group of ex-rodeo stars. Unfortunately, we couldn't get it booked at the same hotel as the show, so it's at a property owned by the company. The winner takes ten thousand dollars to their charity of choice, provided by the studio."

"That's an awesome idea, Blake. I love it. And you know, that's right up my alley. I am a rancher's daughter."

"I can see the down-home country girl in you," he said. "An accident-prone down-home country girl who must have driven her parents crazy."

"My father tried to keep me away from the ranch action," she admitted. "It never worked. Proven by the six times that I had to get stitches."

"You'll have to show me the scars."

She held up her elbow. "That's the only one you can see." She grinned. "Well, when I have my clothes on."

"Like I said, you'll have to show me the scars."

"I'll think about it," she teased playfully. "Did you inherit any of your dad's bull-riding skill?"

"I have an ex-rodeo champion for a father. If I couldn't ride, he'd have had me hung up by my toes for the bulls."

"I've ridden a mechanical bull a time or two," she declared.

"No way."

She nodded. "Way."

"Prove it. If you come to the event and ride, I'll personally donate to the charity of your choice myself."

She laughed. "I'm in. Well, as long as it's not a conflict with filming."

"It's the day after Vegas Week ends."

"Then get your checkbook ready. I'll be there."

"Good," he said, more than prepared to plan six weeks ahead with her. "We can fly out to L.A. together when it's over. Which brings me back to my earlier question. How *are* you handling the flying you're doing?"

She snorted. "Who said I'm handling it?"

"That good, huh?"

"That good." She stopped in front of a building. "This is me. How far away are you?"

"A cab ride," he said, not really wanting to tell her the high-end area he lived in, because it had taken him years of doing his show and investing well to get there. She would get there, too, probably sooner than he had.

"I see," she said, biting her bottom lip and gesturing toward the door. "You want to come up?"

He wanted to come up, all right, and that was a problem. Up meant he was one step away from being inside her apartment. Once he was there, it was all over. He'd forget all the reasons why he shouldn't strip her naked and make wild, passionate love to her. He'd have to survive a kiss. But not down here in the open.

"I'll walk you to your door."

DARLA WAS INCREDIBLY NERVOUS as she walked the narrow tenth-floor hallway with Blake on her heels. It wasn't as if this was the first time she'd been with Blake, but this time felt different. This time not only had she decided to take a chance on Blake, she knew he had taken a chance on her, as well. She'd seen the look on his face when she'd asked who had burned him. And now she knew he was diving into territory he wasn't comfortable in, but that he was doing it for her. She didn't have to know the details. She just wanted to know him. She wanted to understand him. She wanted to wipe away the pain she'd seen in his eyes before he'd looked away.

Her stomach fluttered as she reached her loft's tiny entryway. She reached for her purse, only to realize it was in the bag Blake was carrying. She turned. The space was small. He was big. He was good-looking. He was sexy. She was suddenly burning up, her cheeks flaming right along with the rest of her body.

"My keys are in my purse." She motioned to the bag. "In there."

He shifted the bag from his shoulder to hold it in front of him. She unzipped it and dug in her purse and somehow her shaking hand found her keys. She dropped them and immediately bent down to get them. So did Blake. Their hands touched and they both abandoned the keys.

"Blake," she whispered. "I—"

He snatched the keys and helped her to her feet. "I'll unlock the door for you."

"Okay." Though neither of them moved. A second later he abruptly tossed the bag and the keys to the floor.

His hand slid into her hair at the same instant his mouth came down on hers. She stood on her toes and leaned into him, meeting his kiss with her own. His breath was warm, his body hard. Sandwiched between Blake and the door, she couldn't think of a better place to be in that moment.

The first stroke of his tongue sent a sizzle down her spine. The second turned the sizzle to fire. She was burning up all over again, and he was the only way to cool down. She pressed herself against him, seeking that cool heat. He answered by deepening the kiss and running his hands in all kinds of places she wanted them, needed them. There was a wildness in her she'd never experienced, a hunger only this man gave her.

His free hand skimmed her waist, her breast, her nipple, sending a rush of sensation between her thighs— where she wanted him so very bad right now. Actually, she wanted to get lost in him. Her palms pulled him closer, caressing his powerfully muscled back. Yes. Lost. Please.

Voices suddenly echoed in the building, followed by the sound of keys jiggling in a lock. Blake pulled back, holding himself away from her. His breath was thick, his eyes dark. "I'm sorry, Darla. I didn't mean—"

She leaned in and kissed him. "I did." She bent down and snatched up the keys, then stood again. "Let's go inside." She turned and unlocked the door. Blake stepped in close to her, his hand sliding to her stomach, his lips lowering to her ear.

"I'm not coming in," he said, his voice low and gravelly. "I—"

"You are," she said. "You're coming in." She reached to the ground by his feet and grabbed her bag and shoved it inside, behind the door.

He rested a hand on the door frame above the ringer. "I promised myself I wouldn't do this again until I knew you couldn't write this off as just sex."

Instinct told her that he wanted to know she was taking this risk with him. "There's two of us in this relationship, Blake. And I should tell you right now, you don't get to set all the rules."

He went completely still. "Relationship?"

"Yes. Relationship. You were right, back in Denver. This was never a one-night stand."

"What about the competition thing?"

"You've proven to me that you'll look out for my best interests," she said, thinking of his expression again when she'd asked him who'd burned him. "I hope you believe I'll do the same for you, because I will." She reached out and drew his hand with hers. "I want you to come inside and not for one night. I want you to come inside my life. We'll figure out how to make that work together."

Still, he didn't move, and she started to feel sick, to anticipate rejection. Maybe she'd misjudged this—him, them. Maybe he had simply wanted the challenge of pursuit. The chase. Men liked the chase. He was going to walk away. He was going to leave. She retreated a step, feeling foolish and exposed. And that's when he took a step forward.

16

"BLAKE—" DARLA GASPED as he kicked the door shut and took her in his arms, his mouth soon on hers. She moaned against his lips and desperately tried to resist him, to reason with herself. But when his tongue stroked hers and his hand caressed down her hair, she did what she always did with Blake. She surrendered to what he made her feel, to that unnamed, ever-important something he always made her *need*.

"Whatever you were thinking when you started to back up," he breathed against her lips, "was wrong."

"You—"

"I what?" He kissed her, a deep passionate kiss that must have distracted Darla because she realized they were next to the couch. Again he asked, "I what, Darla?"

The heady masculine scent of him enveloped her, engulfing her in need. "You have this bad habit of having too many clothes on," she answered, shoving his jacket over his shoulders and caressing his powerful shoulders.

Blake caught the jacket at his elbows and reached up to frame her face with hands too big to be so gentle.

"What were you thinking when you backed away from me?" he demanded gently. "I want to know."

Her heart stilled a moment during which she considered avoidance or denial, but she quickly decided against any strategy at all. She didn't want secrets with Blake. She wanted what he had claimed he wanted: honesty.

"I thought," she admitted, "that you only wanted me when you thought I was a challenge. That when I invited you into my life freely, you would no longer want me."

He drew back, slightly surprised. His gorgeous, heavy-lidded eyes probed hers. "No," he said, shrugging his half-removed jacket off and letting it fall to the floor. His fingers framed her neck. "No. That's not the case, Darla. We are so much more than that. You do things to me that I can't even try to understand. I just want to keep feeling them. I want…I need to know I make you feel them, too."

Emotion swelled in her chest. Her hand went to one of his. "You do, Blake. I've just been freaked out because of our jobs and because I… My…" She stopped herself before she confessed her family struggles, her gaze dropping to his chest. There was a difference between being honest and revealing your most personal private secrets. She didn't want him to feel obligated to help or support her because she was struggling. No. Honest was what honest was, but he didn't deserve to carry her family's burden. Still, he just felt so big and strong, such an easily created hero, and it would be equally easy to just let him take care of her. And wrong and weak and…

He drew her fingers to his lips. "Tell me, Darla."

She blinked him back into view. She was tempted by the gentle prod he'd spoken once before back in the hotel, as well, and comforted by the fact that she was certain he wouldn't push her to reply, as she hadn't pushed him earlier on the street. She liked that. She liked that he'd wait on her to be ready, just as he was willing to wait before making love. Not that she wanted to wait. But he would wait—*for her.*

She touched his jaw, letting the light stubble rasp against her fingertips. "I'm just glad you're here, Blake. Right here, where you can be all mine." Her hand traveled the wall of his chest, then she pulled his shirt from his pants. She smoothed her hands underneath, over taut skin and flexing muscle. "Thank you for what you tried to do, but no thank you. Stay. I want you to stay." She nibbled his bottom lip, felt her core clench with anticipation. "I promise to make you as sleep-deprived as I'll be tomorrow."

"I'm not going anywhere," he said, molding her closer with a spray of longer fingers at the base of her back. "Not unless you make me." He leaned in and brushed his lips over hers, a soft caress and a flicker of tongue just past her teeth, a delicious tease as he murmured, "You taste too good." He pushed her jacket over her shoulders as she had his. Darla shrugged out of it and Blake was already pulling her to him again, claiming her mouth with his, making love to her with his tongue, his hands bringing her closer and driving her wild. Need charged every nerve ending in her body.

Darla fumbled with his shirt buttons, eager to touch him, to explore every last inch of his hard, hot body. He seemed to feel the same. He fumbled with her blouse, his anxious touch sent buttons flying. She didn't care. She just wanted skin against skin. He shoved down her bra on one side and palmed her breast, squeezed her nipple, rough but right. Oh, *so* right. Darla moaned with pleasure, covering his hand with hers.

He slipped a hand beneath her skirt, over her lacy thigh-high stockings and then over her bare backside. He moaned at the same time she did, nipping her bottom lip with his teeth. "Darla, do you have any idea how badly I wanted to do this when you were sitting on that desk during the photo shoot today?" His fingers dipped lower, teasing her with how close he was to the wet heat of her core. He lowered his head and she felt warm breath on her neck before his lips brushed her sensitive skin. "All I could think about was how easily I could have just pulled you close and tasted you again. How much I wanted to lick you and tease you until you called my name." He squeezed her nipple, flicked it. "Did you think of me touching you, Darla? Of me tasting you?"

"Yes," she whispered, shocked that she was admitting such a thing, that she had indeed thought those things in the middle of a public place. But she had. Yes, she had. She'd thought of everything, from him tasting her with his mouth on her in the most intimate of ways, to Blake, in all his naked glory, riding her, buried inside her. It had driven her wild. He was driving her wild now. He made her feel free and uninhibited.

"I've waited hours for this," Blake growled huskily. "Hours that I told myself I couldn't have you. Not tonight."

She leaned into him. He was strong and solid, and perfect in ways she couldn't begin to name or understand. He just…was. "I bet you say that to all the women."

His hands framed her face, his eyes finding hers. "Just you, Darla. You get that, right? There's just you."

Emotion expanded in her chest at the unexpected confession. "Good," she whispered, because it was all she could manage to get out before she could even think about perhaps holding back, being guarded.

"I like that answer," he said a moment before his mouth slanted over hers, his tongue caressing hers with sensual strokes that she felt from head to toe. There was something more happening between them than a few wild nights, something that had no place in the midst of their jobs, but she couldn't seem to care.

She lost herself in the sensation of him touching her, barely aware of how her skirt, his as well, even her bra, had disappeared, just as her inhibitions had the instant this man came into her life. There was only a momentary return to reality in which she realized she was giving him total control. That she trusted him enough to allow him to have it. To enjoy his hands on her bare breasts, to cover them with her own and silently beg him not to stop. His lips brushed her ear, his warm breath sending a shiver down her spine, as he repeated, "Are you going to show me what's under that skirt, or leave me in painful anticipation?" He slid her side zipper down.

"I'd say I'd tease you a little but I think that might have to wait until later," she confessed, letting him inch it down her hips. She kicked it away the instant it hit the floor.

He set her at arm's length, his hands resting on her hips. The heat of his sizzling inspection was as arousing as his touch. Her skin flushed and she still felt sexy, and with Blake, it felt good. *Trust.* She felt trust and freedom with him that defied their short relationship. It was the second time she'd had such a thought and it spurred her into action, piercing the protective walls she maintained, making her want to please him. To show him how good he made her feel.

She approached him, her lips parting at the hungry expression she'd captured on his face. Hunger that bled into her, fed her desire, her passion to show him just how much she wanted him. Darla scraped her teeth over her bottom lip.

"Show *me,*" she whispered. Then in a louder voice, "Undress." She leaned against the couch with her hands behind her, comfortable in her nakedness with him. She liked that. She didn't remember ever feeling as playful or comfortable with any man before. Not that there had been many, but then, maybe that was why—they hadn't ever made her feel this way.

His gaze raked over her body and he took a step toward her. She pointed, the corners of her mouth lifting.

"Not until you have undressed. Halfway wasn't good enough the first time, and it still isn't."

He didn't laugh. In fact, he looked like he was going to combust with the effort to control himself, but he stopped and reached for his pants and toed off his shoes. Her hands immediately went to his waist, then slid over his broad chest, and lower still to his cock.

He made a rough, primal sound and reached for her. But she instantly went down on her knees. His erection jutted forward, thick and pulsing, and she wrapped her hand around it, forming a tight grip. She licked the head. "I'm going to show you how glad I am you stayed tonight."

"You did that when you told me to stay."

"Not as thoroughly as I wanted to." She lapped at the head of his cock, swirling her tongue around it. "You like that?" she asked, playing coy.

"Hell, yeah, I like it," he replied, his voice laden with desire.

Now, she felt in control. She licked him up and down. His expression darkened and he let out a long breath. She licked him some more, drawing him in her mouth and swirling. She was teasing him and he knew it. She wanted him to want her so bad that he couldn't hold back.

"You know you're killing me," he ground out, "don't you?"

"How?" she asked innocently, sucking only a few inches of him into her mouth and drawing back.

"You know how."

She drew him into the wet heat of her mouth until she could take no more.

"Yes," he groaned, his hand going to her head, urging her to keep going. "That's good, baby."

The endearment spoken so naturally made her heart flutter. The desperate need in his voice drove her crazy. She suckled him, her mouth and hand pumping him. Her other hand wrapped around him, using that rock-hard ass of his to steady herself. She wanted him to come, she wanted to know she'd taken this man to the brink.

Suddenly though, he pulled away from her.

"Enough," he said. "Enough." He was completely aroused, set on what he wanted. Before Darla could protest, he had lifted her and was carrying her to her bed. He placed her down on the navy blue-and-gray comforter and was on top of her in an instant, settling between her legs.

He rested his forehead against hers. "You smell good."

She laughed. "You suddenly realize I smell good?"

"I always notice you smell good." He smiled. "Now I know you taste good, too."

Her fingers curled on his cheek, heat pooling low in her belly at the intimate words. "I'm not sure I know how to respond to that."

"And that honest answer makes me want to ask you a very serious question."

Her breath hitched and she tried to pull back to see his face. "What?"

"Please tell me you have condoms and they are nearby."

Again, she found herself laughing. "Dresser drawer."

He didn't waste any time rolling off her to open the drawer. She scooted across the mattress, sliding up to his back as he held up the package. "Four," he said, his tone suddenly gruff. "Why are there only four left?"

Darla barely contained her laughter as she reached over and snatched the condom packages from him, nibbling his shoulders in the process. "One is in my purse, silly man. I wanted to be prepared. I was seeing you, after all."

He rolled over and pulled her on top of him. "Is that right?"

There was a possessive quality to his voice, and she liked it. "That," she assured him, "is absolutely right."

"So you thought we might—"

"Yes," she admitted, tearing one of the condoms from the rest and opening it. "I told myself we wouldn't do this tonight, that I should leave them all at home to be sure we didn't." She reached behind her and stroked his shaft, then raised and shifted her body so that she had better access. Wasting no time, she rolled the condom down the length of him—but not without sneaking in one last teasing lick.

"You'll pay for that," he promised, dragging her up his body, the V of her pelvis flattening on his hard length. He claimed her mouth, his tongue catching hers. His fingers glided over her clit, entering the ultrasensitive core of her body.

She couldn't take it. "Blake, please." She reached between them, fisted his shaft and pressed him inside her.

Relief rushed from her lips as he sunk deep within her. "Finally."

"Finally," he agreed.

They stared at each other, both unmoving and breathing together almost as one. Emotion swelled her heart. That something she'd felt earlier was back, stronger than ever.

"I don't know what you're doing to me," he said, repeating what he'd said before, what he'd said in the hotel in Denver. "But don't stop. I like it, and us, way too much."

"Me, too," she agreed, a moment before his mouth closed down on hers. He shifted his hips and she felt him beginning a slow sway that sent sensations exploding inside her. Their rhythmic grind turned into a fierce, wicked passion, like nothing she'd ever experienced. Until they were not just moving together, but practically trying to crawl under each other's skin. She didn't want it to end, but it had to end. Nothing this good could last forever.

Too soon, she cried out as her body clenched around his cock, the spasms shaking her with such intense bliss it almost hurt. He thrust one last time with his fists pressed to the mattress beside her, his head thrown back and his face etched with pleasure.

She smiled, clinging to him, her teeth nibbling her bottom lip. Taking a risk, letting go of a little control, might not be so bad after all.

17

DARLA WOKE IN A DARK ROOM, noting that she was alone. She felt across the bed, searching for Blake and not finding him. Her heart twisted in her chest, memories flooding her mind. This wasn't how she thought the morning would turn out. Not after she and Blake had spent hours talking, exchanging stories about their families, their jobs, their likes and dislikes. And making love. There had been lots of wonderful lovemaking that had eventually led to raiding her empty fridge. Twinkies and Starbursts had been their only hope of nourishment, considering she'd been home so rarely and hadn't bothered to stock up. It had been wonderful. She'd taken that risk with him, she'd dared to let herself be free with him. She'd fallen asleep, thinking that it had paid off with something special—that she and Blake had been special. Instead, he was gone without so much as a goodbye. Suddenly angry, Darla sat up, wearing nothing more than a T-shirt she'd put on when she'd gotten cold. It smelled of spicy cologne, of Blake. She'd trusted him, she'd—

"You're up. I didn't mean to wake you." She blinked into the darkness at him, his silhouette starting to take shape. He was dressed, about to leave, apparently.

"Why are you skulking around in the dark?"

He crossed the small space to sit beside her, leaning in and kissing her, a warm caress of his mouth over hers. His hand smoothed her rumpled hair. "Because you have exactly fifteen minutes until your alarm goes off, cranky, and I wasn't going to wake you for another seven so we could talk. I'd planned to have coffee in hand when I woke you, but it's not quite ready."

Her stomach rolled. "Talk?"

"Can I turn on the light?"

"If you don't mind seeing me look like I just stuck my finger in the light socket, then go for it."

He reached over and flipped the switch on the brown crystal lamp that had been her grandmother's. A dim glow lit the room. Self-consciously, she brushed at her hair, not sure why she cared. If this talk was what she suspected, it didn't matter how she looked anyway.

"You're beautiful," he said, settling down fully beside her. *He* was beautiful, she thought, with all that dark stubble shadowing his jaw, his hair tousled. This was a different Blake than the Mr. *GQ* the cameras saw. This was the Blake she'd come to know last night, the casual, sexy, wonderful man who loved his family, loved his life.

"I'm a wreck," she blurted, and it wasn't a counter to his compliment. She wasn't talking about her looks. He was in his thirties, a bachelor who'd never been engaged, per his prior night's confession. She had a feeling she was about to find out that was because he had a commitment phobia that matched her phobia of flying.

"You're not a wreck," he assured her, curling his hand around hers. "I wanted to talk to you about this before now, but time got away from me. Last night—"

"Was a mistake," she supplied, the words exploding from her lips. "I get that. I understand. You don't owe me—"

"Whoa!" he said, leaning back as if slapped. "What just happened? How did last night become a mistake? Because it sure as hell wasn't for me."

"It wasn't?" she asked, confused, a tiny light of hope forming in her. "But I thought you…"

He arched a brow. "You thought I what?"

"That you were about to say that."

He was still, his jaw set, hard. "Is that what you hoped I'd say?"

"No," she said honestly, unwilling to talk in circles. She wanted to know where they stood. She couldn't take any more uncertainty in her life right now. "You were just up and dressed and—"

He bent his head and kissed her, a tender swipe of his tongue against hers that sent a shiver of desire down her spine. "Do I seem like I think last night, or this morning, or anytime in the future for us, is a mistake?"

No. He didn't. "I'm sorry," she whispered, brushing her hand over his jaw. "Last night happened and now I fly out of town and it's just confusing."

He inched back to look into her eyes. "*Relationship,*

Darla. We talked about us being at that place before I even decided to stay the night."

He's worth taking a risk for, the voice in her head reminded her. "Yes," she agreed. "Relationship."

"Good," he said, pressing his lips to her forehead, his fingers brushing a wild strand of her hair behind her ear. "Which brings me back to where I was a few seconds ago. Last night, when I was hailing cabs for the group to leave the restaurant, Meagan told me that she knows we have something going on, and she's fine with it, with one condition."

"A condition," Darla repeated, her stomach knotting up all over again. She had conditions left and right, and conditions from Meagan were big, because, friend or not, Meagan was her boss.

"This new advertising campaign is being built on the two of us being ratings enemies. The studio is spending a fortune on it and they expect people to be intrigued by our dynamics. Some will watch to see us do battle. Others will hope we end up right where we have. The good news is that us being seen together isn't an issue. It feeds speculation. Being seen together in a way that makes our real relationship obvious is trouble, though, for the show—and trouble for us. We can't let the cast or crew know we're together. It's too risky. People sell things to the tabloids."

Darla wasn't surprised that Meagan supported their relationship after their talk in Denver, nor was she surprised about the concerns. "She's trying to protect the show. I understand that."

"I understand, as well, because she really did dive

in headfirst into making us a ratings grabber for the season. Ultimately, it's exposure for us both. We have to show gratitude for it by making it work. When this season ends, however, we'll have to make it clear we're going public with our feelings."

"Next season?" she asked, shocked that he was planning so far in advance.

He wrapped her in his arms. "Next season," he repeated. "Because I'm pretty sure you're going to make me fall in love with you long before that."

"Love?" she murmured, her heart pounding in her chest. Blake thought he was falling in love with her. "Did you say—"

"Love," he said. "Yes. Do you have a problem with that?"

"No," she replied hoarsely, "I don't have a problem with it at all, actually. But isn't it early to say that?"

"I'm thirty-two years old," he said, "and I've never once used that word with a woman. I don't think I'd call it rushing."

"Never?" she asked. "Not with anyone?"

"Never."

"Not even close?"

He hesitated. "Once. I was young and it's a long story for another time."

"The person who burned you," she said softly, trying not to push. She saw the tension shudder through him and she laid her hand on his leg. "You don't have to answer."

"It's not that I don't want to tell you. It's just not for here and now. I should leave before you do to avoid any prying eyes. That's why I got dressed while you were sleeping."

She shook her head. "I'm not pressuring you."

"I know," he said, cupping her face. "And I appreciate that." He studied her. "What about you? Ever say 'I love you' to a man?"

"There was a college boyfriend I thought I might be headed there with, but it turned out he was headed there with several women who thought the same thing." That was when she'd really learned just how bad a judge of men she really was. But she didn't want regrets or fears to make her lose Blake. If she got hurt, she got hurt. "No one since then. I quickly learned this business is full of men with agendas and I didn't want to be with anyone like that." She pressed her lips to his, knowing the truth—she was falling in love for the first time in her life. "No one until you."

His eyes darkened, his fingers tangled in her hair as he reclaimed her mouth, his tongue brushing hers with tender, passionate strokes that had Darla sighing with the goodness of it—of them, of this new relationship. She was even beginning to think that maybe, just maybe, she and Blake could find that something special that lucky couples, like both her parents and his, shared. And all they had to do to claim their prize was survive the rest of the season.

Two hours later, Darla had showered and dressed in a cotton peasant blouse and soft faded jeans for travel to a series of audition stops that would include Boston and Dallas, then on to Houston. Lugging her carry-on bag in front of her, Darla rushed down the center aisle of the plane to find Meagan, looking panicked, leaning over her armrest to watch for fellow passengers. "I thought you were going to miss the flight," she said, standing up to let Darla slide into the seat by the window.

"Sorry," Darla said. "I couldn't get a cab." She shoved her bag under the seat. "But never fear, I'm here, ready to make your travel experience a memorable one." And tired. So very tired.

"Long night?" Meagan asked, resnapping her seat belt into place.

Darla's cell phone buzzed and she dug it out of her purse before snapping her own seat belt into place. "I could have used a little more sleep, but then, who couldn't, right?" She glanced down at the text from Blake on her phone. Did you make it? Darla replied with Barely. He replied with Pull the shade down. She replied with No. He answered Yes. She smiled.

"Blake?"

Darla's head jerked up at the question. "What?"

"Are you texting with Blake?" Meagan asked, a smile playing on her lips. "Come on. I know you two have a thing going on."

Darla let out a breath. "I don't know how this happened."

"I didn't with Sam, either," she said. "Actually," she lowered her voice. "I thought I'd just have a hot night and get him out of my system. That didn't go as planned."

"Oh, my God," Darla said. "Me, too."

Meagan's lips curved. "I could have guessed that from miles away. So, you're pretty into him, huh?"

She nodded. "I don't know how that happened, either." Her chest tightened. "Meagan, I know how important this show is to you. I won't jeopardize its success. You have my word."

"Honey, I know that. I trust you. That was one of the reasons I so needed you as a judge. I know I can count on you. I know you will do what's right. It's a little piece of sanity for me. It's why I felt so secure focusing on you for this promotional campaign. You're rock-solid. And I don't know Blake as well as you do, but his reputation indicates he's the same."

Her phone buzzed again. Meagan's buzzed at the same time and she laughed as she looked at the screen. "Sam."

Darla looked at her phone, warming inside as she shared this moment with Meagan, as they both returned messages to the men in their lives.

Darla read Blake's text. Trust me. Put the shade down and close your eyes. You're exhausted. You'll fall asleep. Hello? Are you there?

I can't, Blake, she typed.

You can. Do it now before takeoff. You will barely feel takeoff then. Then close your eyes and think about last night. I am.

Darla glanced out of the window and drew a breath before deciding to take another risk, to believe in Blake. She pulled her shade down. She just had to believe she wouldn't crash and burn—with Blake and without.

18

Two weeks after Darla and Blake's New York encounter, which had been followed by daily texting and phone calls, Darla sat at the judges' table in San Diego with morning auditions well underway.

"I do not understand why we let that girl have a Vegas pass," Lana complained of the contestant who'd just left. "She was a moth, not a butterfly."

"A moth?" Darla laughed, not about to let Lana get to her today. She had too many reasons to be in a good mood. Like finally seeing Blake again when he arrived later in the day. Not only that, she'd bought time on her parents' ranch by negotiating ridiculously high payments she'd sworn to her parents she could handle. "Hmm, well then," Darla continued, "I guess I should rebut by saying she's a caterpillar who will become a beautiful butterfly."

"I'm with Darla on this one," Ellie agreed, flipping her ever-changing hair—it was pink and blue today, yesterday it was some form of purple—over her shoulders.

"Butterfly in the making all the way. That girl is going to spread her wings and fly."

"You're always with Darla," Lana sneered. "One might think you have a crush on her."

Ellie grinned and wrapped an arm around Darla. "A *girl* crush," she joked. "I *lurve* her so much." She dropped her arm from Darla. "Sorry, Lana. I just agree with her choices and not yours."

"I guess I have a crush on her, too, then," Jason said, grabbing his cell phone to check his email, as he often did. "I thought that young woman had talent. Where the heck is the next audition?"

"Technical difficulties, guys," Meagan said over a speaker. "Three minutes and we're taping again."

Lana and Ellie started to argue over what made a butterfly. Darla tuned them out as her cell vibrated with a text. She snatched it from the table, expecting a message from her New York producer about a special guest for one of her shows. The text was from Blake instead. I have a crush on you, too.

She blinked at the text. How had he known what had been said? He wasn't supposed to be in until late afternoon. Her gaze jerked toward the door, half expecting him to walk in any second. Blake was here. He had to be here. Was he here?

Her phone vibrated with another message that read Yes. I'm here, as if he'd read her mind. She smiled, liking the way he really understood. This long-distance thing had been good. Instead of heating up the sheets, they'd spent hours just talking, getting to know each other. It was all Darla could do not to push to her feet to leave the room. She was nervous. She was excited. Wait, suddenly, she was *very* nervous. What if their chemistry had been a temporary illusion? What if the magic was gone? What if they'd imagined it in the first place?

The lights in the room flickered and then went dark. "Now *that's* what I call a technical difficulty," Jason commented.

One of the crew announced, "The entire hotel is dark. Meagan says to take fifteen minutes and not a second longer. We have a line of contestants to get through and a plane to catch to Washington for tomorrow's auditions."

Washington. That was where she and Blake were going to stay overnight together, before he went back to New York and she had to go to Nashville. The thought sent her to her feet, eager to freshen up before she saw Blake. She grabbed her purse and excused herself, heading toward the judges' private exit.

She'd never been this excited, and this nervous, over a man before. That had to be a good sign. Please let it be a good sign.

THE INSTANT DARLA REACHED the hallway where Blake was waiting, he reached for her.

"Darla," he whispered, trying not to scare her. He gently pulled her through the door and then behind it, before someone else entered.

She gasped and stiffened, only to sink into him. "Blake—"

He kissed his name from her lips, drinking in her

sweetness and absorbing her soft, warm body into his. His hand caressed her backside over her snug black jeans. She whimpered into his mouth—a sexy, feminine sound that had him wishing they could escape and be alone, where he could hold her, touch her, be with her without fear of observation.

"You feel so good," he murmured. "I missed you."

"I missed you, too." Her hands curled on his chest. "I can't believe you're here. You weren't supposed to be here until much later."

"I finished filming last night and I grabbed an early flight," he explained. "God. You have no idea how much I was looking forward to this, how much I needed to know it still felt this good."

"Me, too," she said quickly. "Oh, me, too." Her hands laced around his neck. "I can't believe you were thinking the same thing. I was afraid it wouldn't feel the same in person as before—as if I'd imagined it."

He wrapped his arm around her waist and pressed his forehead to hers. "It feels better than before. Every time I think I can't get more crazy about you, I do. I cannot wait to get you alone. I'm not sure I can wait until tomorrow night when we're in Washington."

Her hand flattened on his chest. "We agreed to be careful. The judges are always on the same floor."

"I know," he said. "But—"

"No buts." She kissed him. "We wait until tomorrow."

He sighed and leaned against the wall. "I don't suppose this means you'll reconsider the webcam?"

"No," she said tightly. "I'm not—"

"Going to have webcam sex," he finished for her, laughing. "So you told me three times before. But a guy has to try. So phone sex it is, then."

"We aren't—"

"Oh, yeah, we are," he said, holding her close. "And that's just for starters. There are so many things I want to do with you, Darla. You have no idea." And one thing he realized right then and there, he'd already done. He'd fallen in love.

IT WAS NEAR TEN O'CLOCK that night when Blake joined the rest of the cast and crew—a good twenty-five people— in a large room for the big unveiling. Meagan stood at the front of the group beside what looked like a sheet covering a large piece of art on a stand.

"Blake and Darla," Meagan called. "Can you both come up here, please?"

Blake moved to the front of the room, his gaze connecting with Darla's as they both took center stage, so to speak. He could feel the room fill with silent questions and curiosity, as he took a spot on the opposite side of the sheet-covered stand from Meagan. Darla crossed to stand beside him.

"I'm sorry to do this so late," Meagan said to the room. "I'd planned a little party, with cake and champagne, which will now be served on the flight to Washington, if you're awake enough to enjoy it. I have some exciting announcements about this season. Last season we had the curse that haunted the set and boosted ratings."

"And a tornado," someone shouted.

"Yes," Meagan agreed. "And a tornado. It almost makes you believe we really did have a curse. Except that the 'curse' turned into a ratings blessing. I have to admit that I hated that curse at first, and I wanted the show to stay about the dancers. But the truth is that because of that extra enticement, it brought viewers to tune in and gave the dancers the attention they deserved. So. That brings me to this season. Reality shows have become more common now, and the competition is steep. We have to have that extra something that makes each season unique. This season we have Blake and Darla who, as we all know, are competitors in daytime television. So we are going to use that as our gimmick. 'Will they kiss each other or kill each other?' is the concept that will be promoted on billboards and in television spots. Also, the big news that I'm sharing for the first time with Blake and Darla right here and now is that the studio rented Times Square ad space." She pulled the sheet off the display and the room broke into one huge gasp.

Blake and Darla both moved to get a better view of the mock billboard that read The Competition Is Turning Up The Heat On This Season of *Stepping Up*. And there was no question—the picture was hot. It was one of Blake's favorite shots of Darla on top of the desk with her long, gorgeous leg extended, her skirt hiked well above her knee, and her heel pressed to his chest.

Meagan slid between them and slipped her arms around their shoulders. "What do you both think? Pretty cool, right? Times Square, here we come."

"I think I'm blushing," Darla murmured.

"I think *I'm* blushing," Blake said, scrubbing his jaw.

"I know I am," Meagan agreed. "You look hot, honey. Hot!" Meagan darted away and called out to the rowdy, excited room. "Okay, folks. Quickly, so we can get to the airport. We want the press and the viewer to speculate about Darla and Blake. Friends, enemies—"

"Lovers!" someone shouted.

"Oh, yeah," someone else said. "The look on Blake's face in that picture says it all."

Darla's blush had turned to beet-red, and Blake decided he'd take matters into his own hands. "You know how you can find out the truth?" he called out to the room. "Tune in at eight central standard time on Wednesday nights. That's the idea, folks. Job security and ratings. Let's shoot for number one in our time slot!" The room filled with roars of excitement.

"Shuttle leaves in twenty minutes for the airport, folks!" The room started to clear and Meagan rushed toward Blake and Darla. "Even our cast is dying to know what's between you two. I have a good feeling about this." She glanced between them. "They all have confidentiality agreements but that doesn't mean they won't blab. Stay mysterious." She grinned and leaned in, lowering her voice. "You're the only two on your floor in Washington. You can thank me later." She turned and hurried away.

Blake looked at Darla. "I'm never going to stay away from you tonight now, you do know that, right?"

She blinked up at him. "Promise?"

He glanced at the mock billboard, feeling his blood run wicked-hot, and then glanced back at her. "That would be a solid yes on that promise."

Darla and Blake burst into her Washington hotel room in a clatter of luggage, bags and laptops being thrown aside. Locked in an embrace, they were against the wall, then the other wall. Then tearing off each other's clothes. Her shirt, her bra—his mouth on her breasts. She shoved at his shirt. "Take it off. Take it off. Take it all off."

"You, too," he said, nipping her lip.

She backed into the room without really seeing it. A bed. That was all she cared about. She unzipped her jeans and tossed a boot aside. Then tried to tug the next one free, only to somehow tumble to the floor, laughing. A shirtless, shoeless Blake came down on top of her, his long, hard body framing hers. "I feel like I've waited a lifetime for this," he murmured, his lips near hers. His breath was a warm, seductive promise of the hot, perfect kisses she'd been dreaming of for weeks now.

"I do, too," she whispered breathlessly.

His mouth captured hers, devouring her with long strokes of his tongue that had her meeting each one with equal hunger. Her hips arched into him. Even through his jeans, he was hard and thick. She craved the feeling of him inside her. *Finally,* inside her again.

He must have felt the same way, because his hand went to her hips, he started to shove her jeans down without success. He cursed softly out of frustration, which made her smile at his impatience. She knew what he felt. She felt it, too.

He lifted to his knees and half growled, "Raise up, baby." His voice and the endearment were a sexy combination that had Darla smiling. His gaze went to hers.

"Go faster," she said, letting him slip off her pants and her tiny G-string. "My boot is still on." He tossed it and her clothes aside then he stood up, immediately discarding his own pants and underwear. He had a hungry edge to him that she liked more than just a little.

Darla rose up on her elbows, intending to push to her feet, too, but she didn't make it. He was already sliding a condom over his thick erection, his firm body so damn stunning that she couldn't move.

Her throat went dry and she licked her lips. Blake whispered her name and started moving toward her. He bent and swept her up in his arms.

The bed was like lying on a cloud, she thought, as he smiled at her warmly, spreading her legs and settling his thick erection between them. She moaned at the feel of him there, at how much she wanted him inside her. He inhaled and stared down at her. His gaze raked over her breasts.

Darla forgot to breathe for a moment at what she felt with that connection and what she saw in his face—the desire and tenderness she'd never thought could exist in one look. She loved him. She loved this man. "Yes. I like this."

"Good," he said, touching her gently before sliding inside her. She sucked in a breath at the feel of him stretching her, taking him deeper until they were one. His hand went to her cheek, bringing her face to his. "Because I'm glad we're here, too. And I like you in my life, Darla."

A tremor of panic overcame her and she slid her hands to his face. "I like me in your life, too. I like you in mine. So please, don't be the wrong guy."

"I'm *not* the wrong guy," he promised, and then sealed it with a kiss.

It was a long, drugging kiss that took the wildness of their need for each other to another place. To a softer, more sensual place. And when he pulled back to look at her, his eyes smoldering with so much more than heat, she could feel him everywhere, inside and out. She could feel this connection they had growing and shifting.

She reached up and traced his lips. "Blake," she whispered, unable to find any other words to describe what she was feeling right then.

He covered her hand with his and kissed her fingers, before slipping his hand behind her neck and bringing her mouth to his. "This is where I want to be every night."

She smiled against his lips. "Really?"

He brushed hair from her face. "If it's with you."

"Yes," she said, her chest tightening again. "Yes. I want that."

She wasn't sure who moved first, but suddenly they were kissing, their bodies entwined in a seductive, mind-numbing dance, her body tingling and warm all over. Slow turned to fast and wild as their need expanded and took control. They clung together, pressing into each other, trying to get closer.

Release came on Darla without warning, and she tried to fight it, tried to make this last, but it was impossible. She gasped with the sudden spasm of her body, dropping her head to his chest. He moaned near her ear, and she felt him shake against her, felt the intensity of his release. Time stood still until she brought the room back into focus. For what felt like minutes she didn't want to end, they lay there, breathing together, just being together, until he affectionately stroked her hair.

"I have an important question for you," he announced.

She leaned back to look at him. "You say that at the worst times."

"What's bad about me asking you if you want to shower before or after we order pizza?"

She smiled. "While we wait for it to be delivered."

He kissed her nose. "I like the way you think. And once you feed me we can give the bed another whirl."

"Once you feed me," she said, "I might need to give sleep a whirl."

"As long as you let me try and talk you out of that, I'm a happy man." And she was most definitely a happy woman.

19

FOUR WEEKS LATER, WHEN DARLA stepped into the cabin of the Vegas-bound private jet in Dallas, Texas, she found Blake in the second row aisle seat. His brilliant blue eyes fixed her in one of his searing stares that always set her pulse racing and her body flaming. That it did so now, and that she was thinking of the naughty things they had done the night before, was a testament to just how hot and heavy their relationship had become, because she was sick and getting sicker by the second. "There are no other seats open," Ellie said from the front row next to Jason. "You're stuck with Lana."

Darla jerked her gaze from Blake's and centered her attention on the empty seat next to Lana opposite Ellie and Jason. A new wave of nausea overcame Darla, and she sunk into the aisle seat beside Lana, not even caring that Lana would leave the shade up and niggle at her nerves. It was nine o'clock and dark outside and she just needed to sit before she fell.

"I don't know why you and Blake don't just sit together," Lana commented. "We all know you two are an item."

"Sorry, Lana, but you're stuck with me," Darla said in the perpetual avoidance mode she'd been in since the first television commercial had run last week. The feedback from the television blogs, as well as the cast and crew, was buzzing about her and Blake. She kicked her bag under her seat, feeling like she was about to end up there, too, if she wasn't careful, and wishing the bathroom wasn't at the back of the plane.

"You okay, Darla?" Ellie asked, touching her arm from across the row. "You've gotten paler by the minute today and you didn't even try and change seats with me. In fact, you didn't even argue with Lana one time today. I'm worried about you."

"Thanks, sweetie, but I'm just tired," Darla said appreciatively. She liked Ellie, who was truly a nice person.

"You really do look as white as a ghost," Lana said, giving her a keen eye. "Are you sick?"

A ghost. Great. Just what she wanted to look like for Vegas Week. Darla turned to look at Lana. "Why? Are you afraid I'm going to throw up on you?"

Lana grimaced. "Don't be silly. I'm not heartless. I only give you a hard time because you're just so easy to rile up and, let's face it, because I knew the television viewers would love our dynamic—and they do. This thing with you and Blake will be a one-season mystery that can't last. The audience's desire to see us squabble will carry over beyond the season."

"Just remember you said that when we disagree in Vegas."

"I'll show you no mercy," Lana assured her. "For the good of the ratings and job security, of course."

Darla managed a small smile, suddenly liking Lana more than she thought possible. "Of course."

"We'll call a truce for now, though. It's not fun baiting you when you don't respond with appropriate rebellion."

"Truce," Darla agreed, shutting her eyes as they began to taxi, pretty sure the fact that she didn't care when the plane lifted off wasn't a good sign about just how sick she was. This couldn't happen at a worse time. Things were looking positive, but she'd seen enough in this business to know anything could go wrong, and sometimes nothing went wrong and the studio heads still made unexplainable decisions. Having a good audience response to her performance during Vegas Week, and then as she sat at the judges' table for the first four live shows, were critical to assuring her bonus.

BLAKE KNEW SOMETHING WAS WRONG with Darla and it was killing him to sit in his seat and not go to her. He'd tired of this game of hiding their relationship pretty much right out of the gate, but they were bound by their word to Meagan and by the show's ad campaign, and he'd live with it for now.

Darla pushed to her feet abruptly and rushed past him so quickly, he couldn't see her face. He sat there, telling himself not to get up and follow her. Fifteen minutes later, he was too concerned to stay seated. He stood up and Lana turned around, talking to him over the seat. "Yes. Check on her. She's more than a little sick."

Blake didn't reply. He headed toward the bathroom and knocked. "Darla?" No reply. He knocked again. "Darla." He yanked on the door and it opened, unlocked. She was sitting on the tiny space in front of the sink, her knees to her chest and her head on top of them. His heart lurched and he knew she was in trouble.

He didn't even consider how it looked. This was the woman he loved. To hell with charades and ratings. He bent down next to her. "Darla, honey," he whispered urgently, gently pulling her head back.

"Blake," she mouthed in a barely audible voice, her face was sheet-white with black makeup smudges marking her cheeks. "I…"

"It's okay. Don't try and talk. I'm going to find a place for you to lie down."

"No, I can't…move. Too…sick."

"What's happening?" Meagan asked, pushing in beside Blake. "Oh, God."

"Clear the back seats so she can lie down, will you?"

"Yes. Of course."

Blake started to lift Darla. "No. Sick. I'm sick."

"We'll get you a bag," he promised, "but you can't stay on the floor. It's not safe. I can't pick you up in this small space but I'll hold on to you, okay?" He was already pulling her to her feet and she all but collapsed into him, moaning as though she hurt.

Meagan stood in the aisle, her expression worried, as

she indicated the open row. "She needs a bag." Blake managed to maneuver Darla and himself into the seats.

"Bag," she said in a panicked voice. "Bag. Hurry."

The flight attendant rushed up the aisle and handed it to Meagan, who opened it just in time. Blake held her as her body shook. "I can't believe this is happening."

He ran his hand over her hair, hating that the seats were too small for her to lie down. "I know. I'm sorry, honey, but I'm here. We'll get you to a doc when we land."

Meagan bent down next to her. "Is it just your stomach?"

She wet her lips. "My head, too."

Meagan glanced at Blake. "It's so sudden and violent it might be food poisoning."

"Started after lunch," Darla whispered without opening her eyes.

Meagan nodded. "Food poisoning. It has to be. This is too wicked to be anything else." She pushed to her feet and claimed the seat in front of them, so that she could stay near Darla.

Eventually, Darla blinked up at him and whispered, "Thank you for taking care of me."

"You don't ever have to thank me for that."

"Yes, I do." Her lashes fluttered and she fell asleep. He held her for a good forty-five minutes, thankful she was resting.

When they were near to landing, Meagan squatted beside him. "The doctor is waiting on her, but he says if he's even slightly worried about her when he sees her, he's sending her to the E.R."

"I think that's smart." He hesitated, all too aware that everyone on the plane now knew he and Darla were together. "Meagan—"

"If I was this sick, no one would ever keep Sam away from me," she said, before he could say anything else. "I'll talk to everyone about keeping quiet but if it gets out, it gets out. The public is enthralled with the two of you. I don't see that changing."

BLAKE ESCORTED THE DOCTOR OUT of Darla's room, having given his diagnosis of food poisoning and prescribed an antinausea injection that seemed to be helping. Blake returned to find Darla sitting up in bed.

"Hey," he said, surprised. "The medicine must really be working."

She nodded. "It is. I'm a lot better."

He gave her a probing look. "And you're worried about everyone knowing we're together."

"I don't want to be worried. I'm so tired of hiding."

"Agreed," he said, crossing to the bed to sit down next to her.

"I'm glad you were with me," she said. "I am. I just… is Meagan upset?"

"No. She seems to believe we are deep enough into the tease that a happy ending is acceptable."

"A happy ending?"

"Yeah," he said, drawing her hand in his. "If I have any say in it, we're going to have a happy ending." He scooted down onto the bed, and pulled her next to him, curling his body around hers and kissing her temple.

"Blake?"

"Yeah, honey?"

"I really want that happy ending."

"So do I, honey. So do I." Finding Darla had changed him, torn down the walls of distrust this business had created in him, and made him happy. He was going shopping for a ring.

DARLA WOKE IN THE HOTEL BED to realize that not only was she fully dressed, Blake was wrapped around her, also fully dressed. Her chest tightened with emotion. There was something more intimate about this moment than any other she'd had with this man. She was so in love with him. A knock sounded on the door, and he stirred, then called out, "We don't need housekeeping!"

"Good," Meagan called. "Because I don't do windows."

"Whoops," Darla said.

"You're awake," Blake commented with unwarranted surprise.

"You just yelled in my ear," she teased. "Of course, I'm awake."

"And feeling better," he commented, kissing her temple. "Good."

"Hello!" Meagan called.

Blake got to his feet. "Boss lady calls," he murmured, heading to the door.

Darla sat up, pretty sure something had died in her

mouth. She needed a toothbrush urgently and she didn't even want to think about how she looked. If Blake still wanted her after this, he moved way up her ladder to the "keeper" shelf.

"Morning, sunshine," Meagan said, stopping at the end of the bed. "Don't you just look like flowers blooming on a spring day? Or not."

"Watch yourself," Blake warned, stepping by Meagan's side, his hands on his lean hips, his hair rumpled. "She's feeling feisty again already."

"I'd call myself about fifty percent," Darla said, glancing at the 7:00 a.m. time. There was a cast and crew meeting at eight-thirty, and the contestants would all be arriving through the day. "I'll be fine after I shower."

Megan dropped onto the mattress and leaned on one arm. "Today is the least important day. Rest if you need to."

"No," Darla said quickly. "No. I'm fine. I have footage for my daytime show to film anyway."

Blake leaned on the dresser directly in front of Darla. "She's too stubborn to rest. You might as well save your breath."

Meagan glanced between the two of them, and then settled her attention back on Darla. "So then, are you up to a conversation about the show?"

"Actually," Darla said flatly, "maybe I feel sick again."

"Don't start fretting on me," Meagan said. "What's done is done. If your relationship goes public, it goes public."

"But the studio—" Darla started.

"Will be happy if the ratings are good. So far, they are terrific. Which, admittedly, makes me want to string out this tease about you two a bit longer. We're not even into the live shows yet, which is where the dancers get the real exposure and, ultimately, this is about them. So that said, I'm going to warn the cast and crew to stay quiet. They're professionals with confidentiality contracts, and these types of secrets with reality shows are not uncommon."

"Why do I sense a 'but'?" Blake asked.

"The 'but' is this week, contestants are in the same hotel we're at," Meagan answered without pause. "We can't control them like our own people, especially those that Darla doesn't send through to the finals, who might lash out at her. So I think that you two need to stay low-key this week, and then we'll be fine. I want these kids who are dancing their hearts out to have viewers and opportunities, which means big ratings. Last season, the footage in the contestant house was a big ratings grabber." She patted Darla's leg. "So do your casting magic and we'll be set."

Right, Darla thought. Casting magic. She knew she was good at picking talent, but she'd never done it with this much pressure, with the world—including her parents' banker—watching. She glanced at Blake and saw him staring at her. She knew from the look on his face that something was wrong. Meagan rose to her feet. "I'll let you get showered and dressed and see you in a few."

Blake didn't move as Meagan departed. He just sat

there staring at her, and he wasn't happy. In fact, she was pretty sure he was downright unhappy.

"What's wrong?"

"What aren't you telling me, Darla?"

20

"WHAT AREN'T YOU TELLING ME, Darla?" Blake repeated.

Darla swallowed the dryness in her throat. "I don't know what you mean."

"Yes, you do. You're too desperate to keep this job."

"Blake," she reasoned, "this is a big opportunity."

"Yet you say you only wanted to be in casting, that you never wanted to be a star. You know, I've beat my head against the wall, wondering what's kept me from confessing my love for you, but I know now. Something doesn't add up, Darla."

He didn't love her. Or he did. She didn't know, but she was pretty sure that if he did, he was about to talk himself out of it. She moved to the edge of the bed. "Blake. I—"

"Do you remember when you asked me who burned me?"

Her throat was dry again. "Yes."

"Lara Wright."

"Lara," she repeated, feeling stunned. "Wright, as in the movie star?"

"Only, she wasn't a movie star when we were seeing each other."

Darla's stomach tightened. "She used you."

"Right."

She sat there, unable to speak, her mind racing. If she told him about the ranch, would he think she wanted his help? God. Had she told him before, would he have thought she was after his money?

Blake made a sound of frustration at her silence and pushed off the dresser, starting toward the door. "You're not being fair," she shouted, confused. "You're judging me because of her. I'm not her. I'm not."

He didn't turn. "I just need to think, Darla."

His back to her felt like a slap and her eyes started to burn. "*What* is wrong with me wanting this to work out? What is wrong with me wanting to work in casting, which I love, but instead of earning pennies, I get to give my family a better life?"

He turned to her. "Darla—"

"They aren't rich, Blake. They struggle. I have great parents. The best. I want to give back to them everything they've given to me." Tears started to stream down her face. She didn't mean to cry, but she was still sick and she was worried and overwhelmed by everything that had happened. "I'm not Lara, and if you think—"

Suddenly, he was on the bed, on his knees with her, pulling her close. "I'm sorry." He wiped away her tears with his thumbs. "I'm so sorry, Darla. I'm not too much of a man to admit I got scared."

"I'm not her."

"I know."

"No," she said, her heart twisting. "You don't." She pushed out of his arms. She was damned if she did and damned if she didn't with him, and she knew it. He would think she wanted his money if she told him about the ranch. He would think she was about fame if she didn't. In the end, he would turn his back on her and she wasn't turning her back on her family. "I think…we have to get through this season and see where we stand."

"Are you saying we shouldn't see each other?"

"Yes."

How Blake had stayed away from Darla for a full week, he didn't know. But when he walked into the Vegas wrap party on the top floor of the hotel, he had one thing in his mind. He scanned the room bustling with cast, crew and finalists, with tables of food and drink and a busy dance floor, looking for Darla. Ready to end the week of hell that was his life without Darla. A week of regretting he'd allowed the past to taint the present. A week of regretting the moment he'd walked out of her room without fighting for her. When he'd let pride and stubbornness convince him that she'd pushed him away because she didn't think he was worth fighting for, when the truth was, he'd been an ass and he knew it.

He found her standing at a table, talking with Lana and Jason. She was wearing a shimmery silver dress that hugged the curves he'd so intimately admired, her pale, silky hair a mass of silk spraying over her bare shoulders.

Her gaze lifted, sliding over his dark suit before connecting with his, as if she had sensed his presence. And like every other time this week when they found each other in a crowd, which had been often, he felt her tension, her pain and her reserve. It was that feeling, those emotions he felt in her, which had both convinced him she really cared about him, and convinced him how royally he'd screwed up by losing her. The only thing that had made him wait this long to pursue her was his fear that if he pushed her while she was under pressure for Vegas Week, he would end up pushing her away.

He took a step toward her, only to find one of the corporate bigwigs in his path and he was forced to make small talk. By the time he pried himself from the man's grip, Darla was gone. Blake silently cursed, and headed to the table where Lana and Jason were still talking.

Lana looked up immediately. "Oh, please tell me you two are going to make up. The rest of us are miserable with you."

"For once I have to agree with Lana," Jason said, clinking his beer with Lana's and taking a swig.

"Where is she?"

"Hiding in the bathroom," Lana said.

Blake was walking before she even finished her sentence. Blake arrived at the bathroom as one of the camera ladies came out. She nodded at him, as if he'd asked a question, clearly one of the many cast and crew rooting for him and Darla to make up. "She's alone," the woman said. "I'll watch the door."

Blake didn't need any further encouragement. He shoved open the door and went inside, rounding a long hall to find Darla sitting in a lounge chair with her elbows on her knees and her face in her hands. Her head jerked up a moment before she came to her feet.

"What are you doing in here?" she demanded.

"I love you more than you can possibly imagine."

"What?" she gasped.

"I love you, Darla. I've loved you since the moment you fell off of your shoe and into my arms and I'm miserable without you."

Her eyes clouded over and she hugged herself. "It took you a week to decide this?"

"No, honey," he said. "I waited a week to tell you because I want us to get the hell out of here so I can finally spend some private time proving it to you."

She squeezed her eyes shut. "I can't do this, Blake. The timing is wrong." Her eyes were dark, etched with shadows. "I have reasons to need this job and you have reasons to resent that I do."

"Darla, no. I was an idiot. I—"

"Blake," the camera lady yelled from the door. "We have a line out here. Hurry."

"Coming," he called over his shoulder. He searched Darla's face and he saw the decision there, the stubborn decision that said he wasn't getting past no, not without a fight. "You're on for tomorrow's charity bull-riding event. Nine o'clock at the Wind Walker Hotel. Don't be late."

Her eyes went wide. "I'm what? We never confirmed I was doing that. We haven't talked about it for weeks."

He pulled her close and kissed her, slid his tongue past her teeth for a deep, sweet taste. "We just did." He brushed his fingers down her cheek and turned away, promising himself it would be the last time he left her like this.

Blake exited the bathroom to find five women waiting in a line, one of whom was Meagan, who smiled as he walked by, but he barely saw her. He was thinking of Darla's words. *It took you a week to decide this?* Damn it to hell. He'd gambled on timing working in his favor, when instead, it might have been the final nail in his coffin, the fatal flaw that cost him the woman he loved.

RELIVING BLAKE'S WORDS—and his kiss—had kept Darla up all night. By seven, she couldn't take it anymore, so she showered and dressed in her best Wranglers, cowboy boots and pink Western shirt. She told herself she was early to the Wind Walker Hotel because she needed to know what her day consisted of, so she could be prepared, when she knew deep down she wanted to see Blake. She was miserable without him but she couldn't see how they could get past his betrayal, and what she still hadn't confided in him.

She checked into the hotel and soon entered the typical high-end Vegas room, which had a large plush bed and some sort of floral design theme going on with pictures and drapes. In the middle of the mattress was an envelope with her name on it, and she knew the writing was Blake's. Beside it was an event T-shirt she assumed she was supposed to wear. Her heart thundered in her chest as she sat down and opened the envelope.

Inside was a printed formal event agenda and a folded card. She opened the card and a room key fell out. "Room 1212. That's where I'm at and where I want you to be. With me." Darla pressed the key to her forehead and squeezed her eyes shut. He was letting her choose, as he always had. And she had more than a room choice to make. She'd thought long and hard about this. She had two options. Choose to weather this storm with the bank on her own, without Blake in her life. Or choose to tell Blake what was going on and risk being hurt again. There was no in between. Until now, it had never seemed the right time. But now, it was time.

If he loved her, if she loved him, he should be a part of what she had going on. She wanted to tell him everything, to believe he really could see beyond his past, beyond Lara Wright, to *her*. She thought of being on that plane, so sick she thought she'd been dying, and how Blake had held her, how he'd whispered she was beautiful when she'd been a wreck, how amazing she was when she'd felt things were out of control.

Darla scanned the agenda, trying to figure out where Blake would be right now, and it looked like he was doing an opening ceremony at eight. That meant he'd be downstairs, already working. Damn. She was going to go all day with this need to talk to him burning inside her.

Hoping to get lucky, she dialed room 1212. Blake

didn't answer. She found her cell phone and called him. He answered on the second ring. "Darla—"

"Blake."

"Where are you?"

"I'm here. In my room."

"I'm glad you're here."

"Listen, I really need to talk to you and I know you're busy and I can't, we can't, but—"

"We will. I promise. My father is with me. Come meet him." Someone said something in the background. "He says he'll take care of you during the opening ceremonies while I film, and tell you all my dirty little secrets."

Secrets. She swallowed hard. "I'll be right down."

He told her the location and then softened his voice. "I mean it, Darla. I'm really glad you're here." And then the line went dead.

DARLA EXITED THE ELEVATOR and headed toward the busy entrance to the Mountainscape Entertainment Center, which was basically an indoor amusement park and the place where today's rodeo events were being held.

Her heart pounded in her chest as Blake and his father, Nick Nelson, came into view. Their resemblance to one another was obvious. In fact, they were so remarkably alike—both tall, lean and good-looking, both in jeans and their event T-shirts—that it was quite something. And if Blake's father was a testament to how Blake was going to age, Darla wasn't complaining. The man was in great physical shape and wore his gray hair and wrinkles with charm and appeal one couldn't help but admire. But it was Blake she focused on, Blake who stole her breath with his dark good looks. Blake who made her heart squeeze and her body ache. Blake who she loved with all of her heart.

In an instant, the two men spotted her. She opened her mouth to greet Blake's father, when Blake pulled her close and kissed her solidly on the lips. He released her and said, "Good morning!"

Her hand sizzled where it rested on his chest. "Good morning."

Nick cleared his throat. "That's certainly a good way to wake up if I ever saw one."

Darla blushed and Blake slid his arm over her shoulder so she could face his father. "Darla, meet my father, Nick Nelson."

Darla smiled and accepted his hand. "Any woman who can wrangle this bullheaded man here is someone I want to spend some time with. And I hear you can ride a mechanical bull."

Darla's cheeks heated at the innuendo—by Blake's father, of all people. "I have a feeling this is going to be an interesting day."

Blake snorted. "You have no idea." Someone called his name from behind. "Gotta run." He pointed at his father. "Behave." He glanced at Darla. "And don't believe anything he says."

DARLA SAT IN THE BLEACHERS while clowns entertained the crowd and Blake's father entertained her with truly hilarious Blake stories.

"He can't ride the mechanical bull, you know."

"Really? He told me he could."

"You don't see him on the agenda to ride today, now, do you?"

"Actually, I don't," she said. "I just assumed he was busy."

Nick snorted. "His mother rides better than him, though that isn't really a good comparison. His mother is pretty damn good. I wish she could have been here today, but her and her sister are doing a girls' weekend. She does a lot of charity work."

"What kind of charities?"

"She's big into animal rescue."

"My parents are, as well. They have a shelter at their ranch in Colorado. That's actually the charity I want to ride for today."

"Well, isn't that something," he said. "You know, we're looking for a place big enough to house some retired rodeo animals until I can find a permanent location. Your parents have any room at their place? There would be a generous donation to the charity, of course."

Darla swallowed hard. "They have the ranch up for sale right now. So yes, they have room, but I think it would be a month or so before they decide if they are staying or not."

He gave her a keen, way too intelligent look. "So it's for sale or it's not for sale?"

"Where's Darla?" Blake said over the microphone.

Darla jerked her attention to Blake and stood up,

happy for the escape. A few seconds later, she was on the stage with a microphone in hand.

"We hear you're going to ride this here cow today," Blake joked, patting the mechanical bull's backside.

Darla grinned. "I hear you're going to ride this here cow." She patted the metal as he had.

"Oh, no," he said. "You aren't using me to get out of this." He held a hand up to the audience. "Is she folks?" Shouts and cheers followed.

"I'm going to ride because I know how to ride. I hear from a reliable source—" she playfully lowered her voice and whispered into the microphone "—his father, that Blake can't ride."

"Thank you, father dearest," Blake said, waving at Nick in the crowd. "I can always count on you to make me look bad."

"What are good fathers for?" Nick shouted, to have a roar of laughter follow.

Darla walked up to Blake and gave him a challenging look. "So you can't ride?"

"Not a mechanical bull," he said playfully.

The crowd hooted and hollered at that one. Darla looked at the crowd. "Just like a man. Talk big when you can't deliver." She grabbed Blake's hand and slapped the microphone into it and then raised up on her toes to whisper in his ear. "I love you." Then, before he could respond, she sauntered over to the bull to hop on top.

21

DARLA FINISHED HER BULL RIDE to the cheers of the crowd. She'd been nervous and plenty rusty, but she'd done well enough to suit the audience. Blake was there when she finished, pulling her against him to help her down, and holding her just long enough to whisper into her ear, "I love you, too, and you are too damn sexy for my own good."

She laughed, enjoying the moment and not letting herself think about the conversation to come later between them. They felt too good, too right. It was going to work out.

Blake raised his microphone and spoke to the crowd. "Darla and I had a bet, ladies and gentlemen. If she got on that bull and conquered it, which I think we all agree she did, I vowed to personally donate to the charity of her choice. And I'm a man of my word. So, Darla, which charity do you want me to send a ten thousand dollar donation to?"

Darla gaped and spoke to him, not the crowd. "Blake. That's a huge figure. Are you sure?"

"I donate a certain amount of my earnings every year. This time you get to pick where." He spoke into the microphone again. "And your charity is?"

She covered the microphone with her hand. "My parents' animal shelter. Is that okay?"

"Sure it is. What's the name?"

She paused and then spoke into the microphone. "Colorado Angel Rescue."

"Ten thousand dollars to Colorado Angel Rescue," he agreed.

Darla reached for the microphone, her hand folding over his. She spoke to the entire room, but looked at him. "Thank you. Really. Thank you so much. It's a great place that does a lot of good for a lot of animals." She held back her tears. She tore her gaze from Blake's, needing to be out of the spotlight before she made a spectacle of herself—and him. She waved at the crowd and headed for the exit.

BLAKE WATCHED DARLA DASH AWAY from him and knew she was upset, though he had no idea why. The one thing he did know, though, was that he wasn't about to risk her taking off before he could get to her. He quickly announced the next bull rider and headed to the sidelines, where his father was waiting on him.

"I'll take over," his father said, leaning in close to add softly, "I'd gamble on her parents being in some kind of financial trouble and she must not have the means yet to take care of them. I think your donation hit a tender spot, son." His father patted him on the back and headed toward the center ring.

Blake stood there for an instant, shell-shocked as everything came together for him. Darla's desperation to make the show work. Her declaration about taking care of her parents. Her self-diagnosed irrational worry over losing both jobs. Damn it to hell, if he hadn't been so busy looking for Lara in Darla, maybe he would have seen Darla for the great person she truly was.

Blake sprinted through the lobby, heading toward the elevators, impatient to get to Darla's room before she could escape. By the time he was at her door knocking, his heart was in his throat. She either didn't answer or wouldn't answer. Or maybe she wasn't even in her room. She might have left or never really checked in. He pressed his hands and his head against the door, digging out his cell phone to call her.

"I'm here," she said from behind him.

He turned to find her standing there, the room key in her trembling hand. "I got on the wrong elevator and I…" She started to cry.

He was there in an instant, wrapping her in his arms and quickly ushering her inside to sit on the bed. Blake went down on his knees in front of her.

"What aren't you telling me, Darla?" he said gently, brushing tears from her eyes. "What is it that you think I can't handle?"

She inhaled and let it out. "It's not that you can't handle it. It's that you might think I need you to handle it, or that you might think I want something from you because of it. And I don't. I just need to tell you so it's not this grinding secret wearing on my nerves. I…I have it handled."

That one statement stabbed him in the heart all over again. "I made you feel like you couldn't come to me over this Lara thing, didn't I?"

"At first, no. At first, I just thought it was too soon to tell you," she said. "It's a lot of baggage. I didn't want that muddling up where we were—or weren't—headed together. Then, when I was close to telling you, there was the Lara thing, and I thought you might think I had an agenda of some sort. Sometimes I think I should have just told you from the beginning, it wouldn't have grown into such a big issue."

"Tell me now."

She gave a quick nod. "My parents got behind on their bank note for the ranch and they didn't tell me until it was pretty close to too late. I negotiated a ridiculous payment plan to catch them up and told them I was making enough money to cover it."

Another lightbulb went off for Blake. "You're not getting paid well for this show." She shook her head. "Being on a competing network and having the ability to keep my daytime show and film on set meant compromise. SAG minimum wage with a balloon payment bonus if the studio options me for season two. They have to make that decision before the fifth live show."

He leaned back on his heels. "Wait. What? SAG freaking minimum wage? Who the *hell* is your agent?"

"That's not common in this situation?"

"Ah, no." Blake was furious. "You have to do something about this. I'll help you."

Fifteen minutes later Darla had fired her agent and hired Blake's—a well-known industry profession.

Her new agent guaranteed her a better contract as soon as he could contact the studio.

He set the phone on the bed and settled his hands on Darla's knees. "Next problem," Blake said. "How much to catch your parents' note up completely?"

She shook her head. "No. No, I'm—"

He leaned in and kissed her, his lips pressing hers and lingering before he whispered, "Marry me. Then it's our money anyway."

"What?" she blurted, pulling back to stare at him. "Did you…do you…?"

"Yes and yes. And that's the same answer I hope you give me." He reached into his pocket and pulled out the silk pouch he'd hidden there for just the right moment. He removed the sapphire diamond ring and showed it to her. "Unique, just like the woman. This isn't spontaneous, Darla, brought on by some big new revelation. This is planned. This is thought out. *You* are the woman I want to spend the rest of my life with. Will you, Darla James, be my wife?"

"Yes. Yes." She threw her arms around him and hugged him. "Yes. Absolutely."

Blake held her tightly. His woman, his wife-to-be. "No more secrets. We're in this for whatever life throws our way, good or bad, okay?"

"No more secrets," she promised.

He leaned in and took her hand, staring into the beautiful green eyes he planned to get lost in for an eternity. "Shall we seal this deal officially?"

She laughed. "Oh, yes."

He slipped the ring onto her finger.

Epilogue

FOUR MONTHS LATER, on a beautiful sparkling fall day, Darla and Blake were married in her parents' Colorado ranch house. They'd been offered money to televise the event, and they'd declined. The media frenzy over their rumored engagement had not only created huge ratings for *Stepping Up,* it had created a media frenzy they didn't want at their wedding.

Now, with all the guests gone, Darla was still riding cloud nine as she and Blake loaded the SUV they'd rented for the short drive to Aspen for their honeymoon. Watching one of the contestants she'd fought for win the show had been exciting for Darla, especially since the young dancer had scored a role on a new television drama based around a dance team.

Blake slammed the trunk shut. "I think we're all set." His cell phone rang and he snatched it from his belt. "It's our agent."

Darla leaned against the truck, eager to hear what

Jack had to say about their contract negotiations with the studio.

"Hold on," Blake said to Jack, covering the receiver. "He says our contracts for the next season of *Stepping Up* are in and they look good, but he's not happy with the terms for the *Blake and Darla Nelson Show*, and he says he doesn't want to void our individual shows until he has what he wants. He wants to know that we both give him full authority to negotiate while we are gone."

"Go get 'em, Jack," Darla replied, settling her hands on her hips. After the man had not only gotten her back-pay but a raise to boot, she trusted him fully. She'd been learning that sometimes giving away control to the right person was just like having it yourself.

Blake uncovered the receiver. "'Go get 'em' were her words. I'll agree with that. But Jack, don't screw this up." Blake laughed and hung up.

"He told you he never screws up," Darla supplied.

"Exactly."

Darla glanced at the porch where her mother and Blake's sat talking, both with rescue cats in their laps. Blake slid his arms around her from behind. "Our parents really seem to get along."

The front door opened and their fathers appeared, their voices in a heated debate. It seemed to have something to do with how to deal with a fence one of the half dozen horses Nick had brought to the ranch kept jumping.

"Well, they do," Darla said with a chuckle. "I can see why you'd think that."

"That's manly love, honey."

She laughed and hugged him tightly. "How long do you think it will take them to notice that the newlyweds are gone if we leave without saying anything?"

"At least ten minutes." He glanced at his watch. "Starting now." They both took off for the truck and hopped in, laughing as they started just one of the many journeys ahead of them.

* * * * *

COMING NEXT MONTH from Harlequin® Blaze™
AVAILABLE OCTOBER 16, 2012

#717 THE PROFESSIONAL
Men Out of Uniform
Rhonda Nelson

Jeb Anderson might look like an angel, but he's a smooth-tongued devil with a body built for sin. Lucky for massage therapist Sophie O'Brien, she knows just what to do with a body like that....

#718 DISTINGUISHED SERVICE
Uniformly Hot!
Tori Carrington

It's impossible to live in a military town without knowing there are few things sexier than a man in uniform. Geneva Davis believes herself immune...until hotter than hot Marine Mace Harrison proves that a military man *out* of uniform is downright irresistible.

#719 THE MIGHTY QUINNS: RONAN
The Mighty Quinns
Kate Hoffmann

When Ronan Quinn arrives in Sibleyville, Maine, he finds not just a job, but an old curse, a determined matchmaker and a beautiful woman named Charlie. But is earth-shattering sex enough to convince him to give up the life he's built in Seattle?

#720 YOURS FOR THE NIGHT
The Berringers
Samantha Hunter

P.I. in training Tiffany Walker falls head-over-heels in lust for her mentor, sexy Garrett Berringer. But has she really found the perfect job *and* the perfect man?

#721 A KISS IN THE DARK
The Wrong Bed
Karen Foley

Undercover agent Cole MacKinnon hasn't time for a hookup until he rescues delectable Lacey Delaney after her car breaks down. But how can he risk his mission—even to keep the best sex of his life?

#722 WINNING MOVES
Stepping Up
Lisa Renee Jones

Jason Alright and Kat Moore were young and in love once, but their careers tore them apart. Now, fate has thrown them together again and given them one last chance at forever. But can they take it?

REQUEST YOUR FREE BOOKS!
2 FREE NOVELS PLUS 2 FREE GIFTS!

red-hot reads!

HARLEQUIN® *Blaze*™
red-hot reads

Double your reading pleasure with Harlequin® Blaze™!

As a special treat to you, all Harlequin Blaze books in November will include a new story, plus a classic story by the same author including…

Kate Hoffmann

When Ronan Quinn arrives in Sibleyville, Maine, all he's looking for is a decent job. What he finds instead is a centuries-old curse connected to his family and hostility from all the townsfolk. Only sexy oysterwoman Charlotte Sibley is willing to hire Ronan…and she's about to turn his life upside down.

The Mighty Quinns: Ronan

Look for this new installment of The Mighty Quinns, plus *The Mighty Quinns: Marcus,* the first ever Mighty Quinns book in the same volume!

Available this November wherever books are sold!

www.Harlequin.com

HB79723

*Bestselling Harlequin® Blaze™ author Rhonda Nelson
is back with yet another irresistible Man out of Uniform.
Meet Jebb Willington—former ranger, current security
agent and all-around good guy. His assignment—to catch
a thief at an upscale retirement residence. The problem—
he's falling for sexy massage therapist Sophie O'Brien,
the woman he's trying to put behind bars....*

Read on for a sneak peek at
THE PROFESSIONAL

Available November 2012 only from Harlequin Blaze.

Oh, hell.

Former ranger Jeb Willingham didn't need extensive army training to recognize the telltale sound that emerged roughly ten feet behind him. He was Southern, after all, and any born-and-bred Georgia boy worth his salt would recognize the distinct metallic click of a 12-gauge shotgun. And given the decided assuredness of the action, he knew whoever had him in their sights was familiar with the gun and, more important, knew how to use it.

"On your feet, hands where I can see them," she ordered. He had to hand it to her. Sophie O'Brien was cool as a cucumber. Her voice was steady, not betraying the slightest bit of fear. Which, irrationally, irritated him. He was a strange man trespassing on her property—she ought to be afraid, dammit. Why hadn't she stayed in the house and called 911 like a normal woman?

Oh, right, he thought sarcastically. Because she wasn't a *normal* woman. She was kind and confident, fiendishly clever and sexy as hell.

He wanted her.

And the hell of it? Aside from the conflict of interest and the tiny matter of *her name at the top of his suspect list?*

She didn't like him.

"Move," she said again, her voice firmer. "I'd rather not shoot you, but I will if you don't stand up and turn around."

Beautiful, Jeb thought, feeling extraordinarily stupid. He'd been an army ranger, one of the fiercest soldiers among Uncle Sam's finest…and he'd been bested by a massage therapist with an Annie Oakley complex.

With a sigh, he got up and flashed a grin at her. "Evening, Sophie. Your shrubs need mulching."

She gasped, betraying the first bit of surprise. It was ridiculous how much that pleased him. "You?" she breathed. "What the hell are you doing out here?"

He pasted a reassuring look on his face and gestured to the gun still aimed at his chest. "Would you mind lowering your weapon? It's a bit unnerving."

She brought the barrel down until it was aimed directly at his groin. "There," she said, a smirk in her voice. "Feel better?"

Has Jebb finally met his match? Find out in
THE PROFESSIONAL

Available November 2012
wherever Harlequin Blaze books are sold.

HBEXP1112